Grant Cortez w
multimillionaire.

Unlike the rich and famous who had winter homes in the area, his family had their roots in this small town. As wealthy as he was, he preferred the pace of life here to that in the big city, though his business interests dictated that he spend a fair amount of time there.

In fact, he had a business trip coming up he could not get out of. And maybe that was a good thing. He needed to get away from Zoe before he did something they would both regret. He wanted her, but his daddy had a saying and it made a lot of sense. "Don't piss in your own backyard. It kills the grass and gets your boots muddy."

Giving in to his desire for Zoe would be a very stupid thing to do—and Grant Cortez was not a stupid man.

MARRIAGE AND MISTLETOE

When millionaires claim Christmas brides...

Snow is falling, lights are sparkling, the scene is set—for winter seductions and festive white weddings!

Don't miss any of our exciting stories this month in Promotional Harlequin Presents! Available now, in December 2007:

The Rancher's Rules
Lucy Monroe

Her Husband's Christmas Bargain
Margaret Mayo

The Christmas Night Miracle
Carole Mortimer

The Italian Tycoon's Bride
Helen Brooks

THE RANCHER'S RULES

LUCY MONROE

MARRIAGE AND MISTLETOE

HARLEQUIN®

TORONTO • NEW YORK • LONDON
AMSTERDAM • PARIS • SYDNEY • HAMBURG
STOCKHOLM • ATHENS • TOKYO • MILAN • MADRID
PRAGUE • WARSAW • BUDAPEST • AUCKLAND

ISBN-13: 978-0-373-82057-3
ISBN-10:   0-373-82057-7

THE RANCHER'S RULES

First North American Publication 2007.

www.eHarlequin.com

Printed in U.S.A.

Award-winning and bestselling author **LUCY MONROE** sold her first book in September of 2002 to Harlequin Presents. That book represented a dream that had been burning in her heart for years...the dream to share her stories with readers who love romance as much as she does. Since then she has sold more than thirty books to three publishers and hit national bestsellers lists in the U.S. and England, but what has touched her most deeply since selling that first book are the reader letters she receives. Her most important goal with every book is to touch a reader's heart, and when she hears she's done that it makes every night spent writing into the wee hours worth it.

She started reading Harlequin Presents novels very young and discovered a heroic type of man between the covers of those books...an honorable man, capable of faithfulness and sacrifice for the people he loves. Now married to what she terms her "alpha male at the end of a book," Lucy believes there is a lot more reality to the fantasy stories she writes than most people think. She believes in happy endings that are really marvelous beginnings and that's why she writes them. She hopes her books help readers to believe a little, too...just as romance did for her so many years ago.

She really does love to hear from readers and responds to every e-mail. You can reach her by e-mailing lucymonroe@lucymonroe.com.

For Myra...a dear friend and heart sister for more than two decades. You are and will always be a very special part of my life.
Much love, Lucy

CHAPTER ONE

GRANT took a swig from his beer and set the long-neck bottle on the familiar oak surface of the kitchen table. He grimaced. It tasted like swill, and didn't smell much better in his opinion, but it was all part of the ritual.

"Damn it, Bud, this is the third one in two months." His date last night had ended the evening with a *Dear Grant* speech, and he hadn't even been able to work up enough remorse to make her feel properly appreciated.

He'd been too busy trying to control the urge to follow Zoe and the guy on the Harley. He'd been looking after Zoe Jensen for as long as he could remember. Too long to take seeing some leather-clad joker with his hands all over her with any kind of equanimity.

Bud did not answer, and Grant took no offense. He stared morosely into his new friend's beady but understanding eyes.

"Guess you understand, *amigo.* You got dumped too."

Bud wiped his face and stared silently back at Grant.

Grant nodded. "Women. Who can understand them? Even Zoe is like a puzzle with a piece missing lately. You should have seen the loser she was with last night."

Just remembering the thick-necked biker-wannabe who

wore more leather than one of his bulls made Grant's jaw ache. He knew Zoe had been going through some kind of emotional crisis since her dad had sold Grant the family ranch, but he hadn't thought she would take it so far. She did not belong on a cattle ranch and she had to know it. He had expected her to come to terms with that truth by now.

If her recent behavior was anything to go by, she hadn't.

He moved the hamster's cage so that he could put his booted feet up on the already scarred oak tabletop. It was the oldest piece of furniture in a house that had been home to four generations of the Cortez family. Surprisingly, it had survived the decorating efforts of his grandmother, his mother, and then his stepmother.

Looking at Bud, he sighed.

A man who talked to hamsters probably had no room to criticize Zoe's choice of dates. On the other hand, a hamster would make a better companion for her than the guy last night.

Grant stood up and put his now empty beer bottle on the counter. He could not stay still and he did not enjoy the feeling. Zoe had him tied in knots and she was not even his woman. But he felt as possessive of her as if she bore the name Cortez. He only wished he saw her as a sister.

His image glistened in the window behind the sink. He glared at his reflection. Disgusted blue eyes glared back. Almost black hair left a little too long brushed the collar of his denim shirt. For once, he looked like the rancher he was. He spent most of his time in suits, overseeing the Cortez conglomerate, but at heart he was every bit the rancher his Spanish great-grandfather had been.

Ramón Cortez had left his aristocratic roots and the country of his birth to make a new life for himself, and every generation after him had built on his efforts. There was no conceit in Grant's belief that he'd increased the Cortez empire more than any man before him, only simple truth.

His father was a millionaire; Grant was a multimillionaire. Unlike the rich and famous who had winter homes in the area, his family had their roots in this small town. And, as wealthy as he was, he preferred the slow pace of life here to that in the big city, though his business interests dictated that he spend a fair amount of time there.

In fact, he had a business trip coming up he could not get out of. And maybe that was a good thing. He needed to get away from Zoe before he did something they would both regret. He wanted her, but his daddy had a saying and it made a lot of sense: "Don't piss in your own backyard. It kills the grass and gets your boots muddy."

Giving in to his desire for Zoe would be a very stupid thing to do, and Grant Cortez was not a stupid man.

He swung around and faced Bud's cage again. Opening the door, he reached in and took the hamster out. The tiny furball started climbing up his arm. "Do you know what my problem is?"

The hamster did not pause in his ascent up Grant's arm to answer.

"I need sex."

Saying it out loud didn't help, and neither did the idea that Zoe's date might be getting more in that department lately than Grant was.

The hamster shifted his path to climb across Grant's chest, unimpressed with the man's problems. After all, the little rodent had gotten cut off too.

Grant petted the hamster curled up near his breast pocket. "Don't worry, Bud. Zoe'll take you in."

She had a soft spot for animals that resembled a *Double Tuffed* down pillow.

He'd never forget the look on her face the day they'd met. He'd saved her life from a mountain cat, only to find out the reason the six-year-old had been wandering the range was that she had been trying to save her pet cow, Flower, from a stock sale. Her dad had been furious, but had reluctantly agreed to sell the cow to Grant instead.

At eleven, he had given up the money he'd been saving to build a soapbox car to buy that cow. He had learned the lesson well, and he'd been taking care of Zoe ever since.

He put the hamster back in its cage as he heard the back door open. Zoe came into the kitchen with a blast of cold air and a flurry of snow. He hadn't realized it was snowing.

He frowned. "You should have waited to come until tomorrow. Just because your truck has four-wheel drive is no excuse to risk the ride over in the snow."

Zoe pulled off her stocking cap, revealing the silky length of her pretty brown hair. The ridiculous bobble on her hat bounced when she tossed it on the counter.

"I'm not driving my truck." She yanked on one glove with her teeth and shivered. "Something went wrong with the doo-hickey and Wayne has it down at the garage. I borrowed my landlady's compact." She shivered again. "The heat's broken."

Grant grabbed her hand and pulled off the other glove. "What the hell were you thinking? You could have frozen on the way over here." She nearly had. Her small hand felt like an icicle. He chafed it between his own much larger and warmer ones, enjoying the smell of spring she carried with her, even in the dead of winter. "Angel, you need a keeper,"

Zoe smiled up at him and her chocolate-brown eyes twinkled. "I already have one. You."

He did not smile back. "I'm not doing a very good job if you're out driving in the snow in some broken-down car without a heater, *niña*." No way was she driving home in that death trap.

She pulled her hand from his grip and started unbuttoning her coat. Her fingers trembled. "I'm not a child, and the car isn't broken—just the heater. What's the emergency?"

He picked up the hamster cage. "This is the emergency."

Zoe's eyes narrowed and she crossed her arms over her chest, pressing the swell of her breasts against her loose knit sweater. "No."

Ignoring his body's blatant reaction to the subtle stimulus, he forced his gaze to her less than welcoming expression.

She stomped her foot and snow fell onto the kitchen floor. "Do you hear me? I'm not taking him."

Grant opened the cage and pulled the hamster out. He extended his hand to her. "Look at those sad little eyes. He's already been rejected by one woman. Don't do this to him."

She did not take the animal, but stood defiantly silent— all five feet two inches of her.

"He was a gift to my foreman's daughter, along with another hamster. The pet store said they were both female."

Zoe's eyes widened in comprehension. "They weren't, and your foreman did not want a zillion hamster babies running around the house?"

Grant nodded. "Little Sheila had to choose between her two hamsters. She chose the female. Bud got left out in the cold."

Zoe unclipped her long brown hair and smoothed it back, clipping it again. Grant recognized the gesture. She was thinking. She looked at him, her expression unreadable, and then shifted her gaze to the hamster. She reached out to take Bud and cuddled the little furball close to her chest.

Her nicely rounded, high-breasted chest. He ground his teeth at the thought. He hadn't noticed Zoe's feminine attributes since the summer she was nineteen—he'd made sure of it—but lately his body had been going haywire around her. He definitely needed an outlet for his libido.

"What's his name?" she asked.

"Bud."

"Why didn't they just take him back to the pet store?"

"They tried, but the store owner wouldn't take the older hamster along with the babies."

Zoe's gaze shot to his. "They already had babies?"

"Yep. That's how they figured out they weren't both females."

Zoe raised her brows at this. "They couldn't figure it out before that?"

Grant shrugged. "I guess not."

"Why can't you keep him?"

"Get real. I don't do small furry animals. That is your domain. I do not begin to have time for a pet." Not even a hamster. "Besides, I have to fly out for a business trip tomorrow."

"So, me coming tomorrow would not have worked?"

"No, but had I known you planned to take your life into your hands to make the trip, I would have come to you."

"Bringing Bud, no doubt."

He did not bother to answer. That was a given.

Her eyes skimmed the kitchen, another indicator that she was thinking heavily, and her gaze lit on his empty beer bottle. "Get dumped again?"

"Don't sound so cheerful about the prospect."

"The woman last night? Linda?"

"Yes."

Zoe smiled. "She take exception to you turning your evening into a double date at the last minute?"

As a matter of fact, she had. But Grant wasn't about to share that with Zoe. He shrugged instead.

She laughed. "You didn't have to join me and Tyler. He's a sweetheart under all that leather."

"Sweethearts do not get tattoos of naked women in chains on their biceps."

Zoe had got that *I'm going to protect the underdog* look on her face. "He got the tattoo when he was a lot younger. You shouldn't judge a man by the vagaries of his youth."

Grant couldn't help it. He laughed. Zoe leaping to the defense of an abandoned kitten made sense. Zoe protecting the reputation of the guy she had been out with the night before did not. He had looked like someone who could take care of himself and Zoe besides. That was why Grant had insisted on joining them. He hadn't liked the way the other man had looked at her.

"You going out with him again?"

She shrugged. "I don't know. Maybe."

"Come on, *niña*. He's not your type."

She looked at him, and something in her eyes made his body tense, ready to do battle. "Just what *is* my type, Grant?"

"It's not that clown from last night."

She walked over to the table and gently put Bud back in his cage. "His name is Tyler."

"I don't care what his name is. He is not the right man for you."

"Yeah, well, according to you, neither are any of the other men I've dated since I was sixteen."

It was an old argument and Grant knew he'd lose. Zoe dated who she wanted, driving him crazy in the process.

She grabbed her coat. After she'd put it on, she yanked on her gloves and hat. The bobble bounced wildly from her harsh tugging. "I'm really not in the mood to argue about this. I've got forty little yellow bells to cut out for tomorrow's craft project. I'd better be getting home."

Grant grabbed his car keys from the drawer by the sink. "Take my truck. You don't want Bud to freeze."

She considered his suggestion silently. He could tell she was warring with her desire for independence and her concern for the hamster. "What about my landlady's car?"

"I'll follow you and drive my truck back."

She chewed on her lower lip. "It's a cold ride. Mrs. Givens doesn't need the car right now. It belongs to her son and he's away at college. Just bring it by when you get back from your trip. I assume you are flying out in the morning?"

"Yes."

"You could have one of your hands make the transfer tomorrow, if you like."

"We'll see," he said noncommittally, knowing he would not do so. He would rather she kept his truck until his return, when hopefully her own vehicle would be repaired. He was careful not to let the satisfaction he felt show in his face, however.

If she thought he was getting away with being "overly protective", as she called it, she was stubborn enough to insist.

That Sunday, Zoe rushed around her apartment before Mrs. Givens arrived for tea. She had invited her landlady the previous week and didn't want to cancel at the last minute. It would make the older woman suspicious. Zoe didn't want Mrs. Givens to realize that she had taken in another stray. Even this close to Christmas, she had the feeling that one more pet would prompt an eviction notice.

She led her German Shepherd, Snoopy, into the back bedroom and shut the door, and then tucked Bud's cage into the cubbyhole above the sink in her tiny bathroom. That should do it. With luck Zoe would find a new owner for Bud before Mrs. Givens was any the wiser. The hamster's exercise wheel squeaked as Bud's short rodent legs trod a constant rotation on the plastic device. Princess, one of Zoe's cats, watched with a hungry look. Zoe tapped the acrylic cage and smiled. Even Princess could not get into the hamster's haven.

Just to be safe, she shooed the cat out of the bathroom and shut the door. The doorbell rang and Snoopy let out a shattering series of barks. She hushed the dog before opening the front door, and almost fell backward as she came face-to-face with Grant's imposing six-foot-two-inch frame.

He reached out to steady her. "You okay?"

"Sure." She'd just been expecting a rather short, rather round older lady rather than his well-muscled, ultra masculine person. She'd done a pretty good job of sublimating her body's response to Grant since that awful night when she'd been nineteen, but every so often feelings she'd rather not acknowledge leapt past her defenses. Like now.

"What are you doing here?" Her breathless voice gave her away, but if Grant followed past patterns he wouldn't notice.

Sometimes she wondered if he thought she was as sexless as he wanted her to be. Not that she wasn't, but she shouldn't be, darn it. And that wasn't going to change any time soon. Not as long as her body still thought Grant was *the one,* even if her mind and her heart now knew better.

"I have come for my truck."

"I thought one of your hands would come for it." She frowned in consternation. She hadn't been mentally prepared for a confrontation with Grant right now, even a pleasant one. Not when she needed all her wits to make nice with her increasingly annoyed landlady.

"Still mad I called your boyfriend a clown?"

"I'm not mad, just busy." She forced a smile.

She hadn't been angry the other night either. Not really. Grant couldn't help being overprotective. Besides, she wasn't really dating Tyler, just trying to fix him up with a friend of hers from school. They were both skittish. "Mrs. Givens is coming for tea."

Grant leaned down and scratched the silver fur on her cat's neck. His lean, tan fingers moved in a mesmerizing rhythm, a rhythm Zoe had an overwhelming desire to experience herself. She tamped down the feeling, just like she'd been doing with similar desires for the past four years—longer if you counted how long she'd wanted Grant before *The Night.*

He straightened and dropped a set of keys in Zoe's hand. "She'll be happy I brought back her son's car."

His fingers brushed her palm and she jerked her hand back at the contact. Darn. She needed to get some perspective here. She turned around too quickly and nearly went sailing when her feet got tangled with Alexander, Princess's brother. She yelled. Grant gripped her shoulders and pulled her toward him. She landed against his chest. Still standing, but barely.

Snoopy's barking, the parrot's screeching and Grant's

laughter faded as Zoe became aware of the feel of Grant's hard chest against her back. What would he do if she turned around and kissed him?

Would he open his lips over hers and let her taste his tongue like he had that one time when she'd discovered passion included a whole lot more than the rather innocent dreams she'd been weaving around Grant since she was sixteen? More likely he'd think she'd gone nuts. And she had if she was contemplating giving Grant another run at her heart.

She trusted him with her life, and always would, but her emotions were a different matter entirely.

The sound of another voice alerted Zoe to her landlady's arrival; she jumped away from Grant. This time she watched where her feet landed and managed to stay upright. "Mrs. Givens. Grant was just returning your son's car."

The elderly woman smiled and patted Grant's cheek with her fleshy pink fingers. "Dear boy. You are so very thoughtful. I'm sure we would not have missed the car if you had waited until the weather improved before returning it."

Grant turned his smile on Mrs. Givens and Zoe was able to collect herself enough to find his truck keys. "Here." She handed him the keys. "We won't keep you. I know you have better things to do than stay and have tea with us."

For whatever reason, her hormones were in overdrive today, and no way could she handle Grant's presence at her tiny dinette table. Mrs. Givens frowned at Zoe.

Grant just winked. He really wasn't fond of Zoe's landlady. "As always, my schedule is full."

She knew it was true, and didn't understand why he had come to bring the car back himself. "Then I guess you had better go." Zoe pushed him out the door. "I'll talk to you later."

She closed the door on his rather astonished expression and turned to Mrs. Givens, who was trying to avoid stepping on one of the cats and frankly doing a better job of it than Zoe had earlier.

She smiled at Zoe. "That Grant Cortez is such a nice boy. I remember we all worried when his daddy put him in charge of the ranch at such a young age, but he's certainly made a success of it."

"Yes, he has." Not to mention his other business interests. She often marveled at the fact that their friendship had survived childhood.

Zoe wasn't in a league with the Cortezes of the world any more than she was with the famous actors who now made up a good part of the winter and summer population of Sunshine Springs. It was the new Vale—only more exclusive in some ways, since many of the families had lived in the area for generations and land was hard to come by.

Grant had been forced to pay her father premium rates for the ranch when it had been sold because an actor, a rock star and another cattle conglomerate had all been bidding on the property at the same time.

"Still, a young man at twenty-two should have been dating, not running a spread the size of the Double C." Mrs. Givens tsked her disapproval.

Zoe agreed, knowing better than anybody what it had cost Grant to take over the ranch at age twenty-two, leaving his dad and stepmother free to move to Portland like Lottie had wanted. He'd given up his plans for a career on the east coast and lost his fiancée all in one devastating blow.

He'd resurrected the career, on his own playing field… but not the relationship. And he hadn't had another serious one since.

"Not that he hasn't done his share of dating these past six years. He's very photogenic." Which was the older woman's way of alluding to Grant's many pictures in the press with the supermodels and actresses who graced his arm socially.

Linda was the daughter of an aging rock star who'd breezed into town and thought nothing of dating the area's most eligible bachelor…until he'd gone into "protect Zoe" mode.

Mrs. Givens smiled conspiratorially with Zoe. "I'm sure you know more than the tabloids even…"

The woman was an inveterate gossip, and Zoe had no intention of responding to the thinly veiled hint to share what she knew of Grant's lovelife.

"It's to be expected, I suppose." She ushered her landlady to the table, where she had already laid out the tea things. "I'm trying a new apricot blend tea. I hope you like it."

"That sounds lovely, dear." Mrs. Givens was a true tea connoisseur. She went to sit down and an ear-splitting yowl assaulted Zoe's ears. Alexander must have been sitting on the chair again.

Mrs. Givens shot up from the chair, stumbled one step forward, and fell over Princess. She gasped and crashed to her knees on the carpet. Her blond wig went askew and her thinning gray hair stuck out on all sides. Her polyester dress rode up so that the tops of her knees were exposed, and nausea climbed up Zoe's throat.

Not today. The tea had been an attempt to stay on the good side of her landlady, but now disaster loomed darkly on Zoe's horizon. Feeling doomed, she rushed to the woman's side and lifted Mrs. Givens to her feet. "I'm so sorry. Are you all right?"

The older woman took several gasping breaths. "I… I…"

Zoe pushed her into the now empty chair. "Sit down. I'm sure you will feel better in a few minutes." She patted Mrs. Givens shoulder, not at all sure the older woman would feel better in the next millennium. Her expression was not promising. "Let me pour you a cup of tea."

Mrs. Givens nodded, causing her wig to tip further over her left ear. "A cup of tea. Yes. That would be nice." She rose unsteadily to her feet. "But first I think I'll freshen up in your powder room."

"Certainly." Zoe helped Mrs. Givens to the closet-sized bathroom—remembering the hamster hidden in there only when a truly awful sound emerged from behind the closed door.

The landlady came tearing out of the bathroom, her eyes wild. She pointed a trembling finger at Zoe. "You have a rodent in your…your…"

"His name is Bud. He's a hamster. While technically still rodents, hamsters are domesticated and quite safe as pets."

The expression of horror convulsing Mrs. Givens' features didn't auger well for Zoe's chances of explaining her way out of the situation. She tried anyway. "Please. It will be all right. Bud is harmless."

Mrs. Givens shook her head violently, causing her wig to fall to the floor. Princess and Alexander immediately attacked it with all the fervor of hunting felines left in a cramped apartment for too long.

"My wig," Mrs. Givens wailed. Her hands flew to her head as she tried to hide the gray and white hair.

Wanting to cry, Zoe jumped to the rescue of the wig. She wrested it from the two cats and handed it to Mrs. Givens, who yanked it back on without much improvement in her appearance.

She stood up, trembling with indignation. "I have been more than tolerant."

"Yes," Zoe hastened to agree.

"I have put up with large dogs, screaming parrots, annoying cats, and even allowed you to keep your goat in the old chicken coop. But I will not stand for rodents."

Zoe didn't know what to say. Everything her landlady said was true. "I'm going to try to find a home for him. It won't take me very long. Children love hamsters. I'm sure one of my students will be happy to take Bud home as a pet."

Their parents would be even happier to get the paraphernalia that went along with a hamster for free.

Mrs. Givens sadly shook her head. "I know how much you love your animals, dear. But I simply will not abide a rat living in my home. Even if you found a home for him today, I would not feel safe. Who knows what you would bring home next?" She shuddered delicately. "You might even take it into your head to adopt a snake."

"I truly am sorry. I didn't realize you had such an aversion to rodents. I won't bring any more home. I promise. As for snakes—even I draw the line at reptiles."

Well, that wasn't strictly true, and she was hoping Mrs. Givens had forgotten the iguana incident. The landlady's narrowed eyes told her she hadn't.

"I seem to remember a very reptilian creature living in your bathtub not a month ago. I'm very sorry, Miss Jensen, but you are going to have to find another place to live."

"Please give me another chance," Zoe pleaded, "It's so close to Christmas. It's almost impossible to find living quarters in Sunshine Springs." Especially those that allowed pets.

Mrs. Givens' expression softened, and Zoe would have

been home free if Snoopy hadn't perpetrated his trick of opening doors and come bounding down the hall. Mrs. Givens was not fond of large dogs, and she found Snoopy intimidating. Unfortunately, Snoopy adored her. He jumped up on Mrs. Givens to give the landlady a kiss goodbye.

Zoe shouted, "Down, Snoopy."

The dog obeyed, but the damage was done.

Mrs. Givens wiped the dog slobber from her face, her expression murderous. "The time has come for you to find a home more amenable to your soft spot for animals."

CHAPTER TWO

Zoe rang Grant's doorbell.

It was a new experience.

So was coming in through the front door. She took in the different perspective of the imposing portico while she waited for Grant to answer. Snow covered the ground around the impressive Spanish-style mansion with Christmas-card loveliness. The house was old for the county, probably the oldest one within a hundred miles, and still the most impressive. Wrought-iron grillwork decorated every window and doorway, while the stucco glowed in the moonlight.

She took a deep breath of the frosty air, the faint scent of wood smoke teasing her nostrils. Grant must have built a fire in one of the many fireplaces. Probably the study. She could certainly stand being in front of that fire right now. She shivered and clapped her gloved hands together. *Where are you, Grant?*

She heard a bump and a muffled curse. The door opened. Grant's dark hair stood on end, and the imprint of three fingers marked his cheek. He'd been asleep, but he wasn't undressed so he hadn't gone to bed. He'd probably fallen asleep in front of the computer again. The man worked much too hard.

His comical look of disbelief nearly sent Zoe over the edge into hysterical laughter. Although nothing about this situation was even remotely funny. She lifted her hand and wiggled her fingers in a quick wave. "Hi."

Brilliant. *Hi.* That was really going to convince him to let her stay. She had to look pathetic. She tried.

Grant squinted at her. "Something wrong with your face?"

She sighed. Of course she couldn't do a good job at pathetic. It wasn't in her nature. Grant was the only one who thought she needed a full-time keeper.

"Mrs. Givens evicted me."

How was that for pathetic?

Grant did not say anything. Zoe tugged at the ends of her wool scarf. "She detests rodents. Who would have guessed?" This time she tried for a look of innocent confusion. When Grant just stared at her, she gave up. Frustrated, she demanded, "Say something."

"You rang the front doorbell."

Zoe looked into Grant's eyes. Were they bloodshot? She didn't think so, but it was hard to tell with the hall light off. The outside light was on a timer, but its glow didn't reach far into the entry hall.

"I know I rang the bell." She sighed. "It seemed appropriate."

Grant rubbed the back of his neck. He always reminded Zoe of her father when he did that. She frowned.

"Why?"

"It just did." She chafed her arms and stamped her feet. "I thought you should have some say in the matter, after all."

"Some say in what matter?"

"This matter." Hadn't he heard her say that she had been evicted? "The *I brought one too many animals home and my landlady evicted me* matter."

Grant straightened. "I heard that part. But why ring the front doorbell?"

Couldn't he think of anything besides the stupid doorbell? "Grant, I need a place to stay until I can find a home for me and my pets. I've tried everywhere in town and no one would even consider renting to me."

It hadn't been easy coming to Grant. Not that she didn't think he'd want to help. She knew he would. But she'd been making it on her own, proving that her parents selling off her home and defecting to Arizona did not matter. She'd refused Grant's offer to let her continue living in the family home. Even paying rent it wouldn't have felt right. She couldn't afford the kind of rent the place would have gone for on her salary as a kindergarten teacher, and wouldn't allow Grant to offer it to her for less than the going market rate.

She'd come very close to regretting that decision today.

"One apartment manager laughed so hard when I told him how many pets I had that I'm sure he had a seizure." Zoe's lips were getting numb. "Doesn't it cost an awful lot to heat up the outdoors with your one little furnace?"

He got the hint. Stepping back, he waved her inside. "Come on in. We can talk about your situation in the house."

"I've got to get everyone else." She turned around and headed to her truck. Wayne at the garage had fixed the doo-hickey and it ran better than new. She lifted the canopy window and called back over her shoulder. "The cats are in the cab. Would you get them, please?"

She ignored Grant's less than pleasant rejoinder.

He came out of the house just as Zoe led Snoopy inside,

carrying her birdcage and Bud's home. Grant took one look at her pets and grumbled, "I thought you would take care of Bud, not show up on my doorstep with a zoo."

She smiled. "Consider it a return on your investment."

He frowned at her before opening the cab door. He pulled out the cat carrier. Zoe went around to the back of the truck to get Maurice. The goat had not liked the ride out to the ranch. She pulled him toward the house. "Come on, Maurice, you're going to like Grant's place. It's warm and cozy."

"And it is not open to goats. He can stay in the barn."

"But Grant…" Zoe let her words trail off at the implacable set of Grant's features. At least he wasn't sending *her* to the barn. "Let's go, Maurice. I'll get you some nice, snuggly hay to curl up in."

Grant snorted.

Zoe led Maurice to the barn and settled him in as quickly as possible. She didn't even stop to visit with the horses on her way out. Coming in through the back door, she felt warm air blast her. She looked around the kitchen. Grant had already put the teakettle on to boil. Smart man, not to mention self-sufficient. He kept a minimum of domestic staff, and none of them stayed over in the house.

Though the foreman's wife did most of the housework and cooking, she lived with her husband in a house on the ranch.

Grant turned toward her and she nearly went back out the door. His expression could have tamed a grizzly. It didn't take long for Zoe to get miffed herself. *Some friend.* She could not help it that she did not have a place to live. A tiny voice reminded Zoe that she could have refused Bud. *It was Grant's idea,* she retorted to her conscience.

"I put your suitcases in my old bedroom." He did not sound nearly as mad as he looked.

"Thanks." She gave him a tentative smile. "I really appreciate this, Grant."

"What happened? When I left, you and Mrs. Givens were sitting down to tea. I can't believe she would evict you this close to Christmas."

"Mrs. Givens hates rodents."

Grant's expression did not lighten. "Bud is a hamster."

He was annoyed with *Mrs. Givens.* Zoe should have realized sooner, but she'd been in panic mode ever since her eviction notice.

"Hamsters *are* rodents."

"Why didn't she just tell you to get rid of the hamster?"

"She hit the end of her rope with me, I guess. Said she thought the next thing I'd bring home would be a snake. She never got over the iguana in the bathtub."

Grant narrowed his eyes. "What about your classroom?"

Zoe pictured the look on her principal's face if she showed up with another animal and laughed. "I already have more class pets than any other kindergarten teacher this side of the Cascades."

"I still don't understand why she would just kick you out like that. You have rights. Besides, Mrs. Givens likes you."

"Snoopy kissed her."

Grant's eyes widened, and then he laughed.

Zoe smiled, feeling hopeful for the first time since getting evicted. "I'm glad you find it amusing. Mrs. Givens didn't. She thought it was time for me to find a place to live that would accept my weird need to have so many pets."

Grant's laughter dried up like a creek bed. "She said your tender heart toward animals was weird?"

The teakettle whistled. Zoe scooted around Grant to move it off the burner. "No, she didn't call me weird. She didn't have to. Grant, most people think my tendency to collect pets like other people collect dust bunnies is a bit strange."

"There's nothing strange about it. You have a soft heart, that's all."

"Tell that to my dad." She hadn't meant to say that. She didn't like to dwell on her relationship with her dad. He had never understood her, and she was not sure she would ever understand him.

Grant squeezed her shoulder. "I did."

"Yeah, I know. Always my protector."

Grant brushed a finger down her face. It took every speck of self-control she had not to lean into his touch.

"Always." The warm promise in his voice soothed her.

"So, I can stay?"

Grant stepped back. "We'll start looking for a new place for you tomorrow."

Zoe frowned. "What's the rush? Can't we wait until after the holidays?"

It would be perfect. She and Grant could entertain their parents together, and she would not have to spend any time alone in the company of her father. With Grant around, even Zoe's mom would not be able to finagle such a meeting.

Besides, finding a place wasn't going to be all that easy. Hadn't he heard what she'd said about already looking? She hated facing it, but she'd have to get rid of the goat and the parrot. Someone might rent to her with a dog and two cats, but even that was pushing it.

Grant shook his head. "This is Sunshine Springs, not Portland. Among the year-round residents, kindergarten teachers don't cohabitate with men—not even their best friends."

"We wouldn't be cohabitating. I'm just staying here until I can find another place."

He reached around her and started mixing two mugs of hot cocoa. "You and I know that, but the busybodies of Sunshine Springs don't."

"But—"

"No buts." He handed her a cup of hot cocoa. "I know what we'll do."

Zoe took a sip of sweet, steaming beverage and waited for Grant to tell her about his brainstorm.

"Frank and Emma Patterson went across the mountains to Portland to visit family for the holidays. My ranch foreman is keeping an eye on the place. I'm sure they won't mind if you stay there while you're looking for a new home."

Zoe rolled her eyes. "Yeah, right. Grant, most people wouldn't let me stay at their home with all my pets. Why do you think it's so hard for me to find a rental?"

She also didn't know how she felt about staying in her old home, now occupied by the Pattersons, a wealthy retired couple who rented the place from Grant.

"I'll call Frank in the morning," he said, just as if she had not spoken.

"If you are that intent on getting rid of me, go ahead and call." She set her half-finished mug by the sink. "I'm going to bed. It's been a long day."

Grant frowned. "I'm not trying to get rid of you. The Patterson place is a lot closer to town, and you won't have to drive so far on icy roads to work."

School let out in a couple of days, and Grant knew it. "So, we don't tell anyone I'm staying here. If they don't know, their overstimulated imaginations won't have any fodder. And with school letting out soon, how is anyone going to know?"

Grant's granite-like features twisted into a cynical smile and his blue eyes mocked her naïveté. "Mrs. Givens."

"You think she'll tell?"

His derisive laugh was answer enough.

"Okay. Call the Pattersons."

Grant savored the quiet of the predawn darkness. He'd wanted to make some international business calls before waking Zoe. They needed time this morning to take care of her homeless situation. If she had let him rent her old home to her, none of this would have happened. But Zoe's pride was only exceeded by her stubbornness.

When he walked into the kitchen, not only was the coffeepot on and giving off a terrific aroma, but Zoe was making breakfast. She flipped a golden pancake off the griddle onto a plate. A pan of eggs warmed on the back of the stove. He knew better than to look for bacon.

Zoe was a vegetarian. Ever since she was sixteen and had told him that every time she bit into a hamburger she saw the soft brown eyes of a cow. When she'd said it, he'd come close to giving up beef too.

A vegetarian rancher. Right.

Her dad had gone ballistic. Jensen had never even considered leaving the ranch to Zoe, and when he'd decided to retire early he'd sold the ranch to Grant to add to the Cortez holdings. Her dad had not believed that she would be able to raise cattle to butcher or sell. Grant did not doubt the older man had been right.

Zoe did not belong on a working ranch and that was a fact.

At least she still ate eggs. His stomach rumbled at the sight of the fluffy yellow pile of scrambled eggs on the plate.

"Mornin'."

She turned around and smiled at him. "Mornin'. I made breakfast."

"I see. Are you saying that if I let you stay here I can figure on the services of a housekeeper?" He teased. "That might make me rethink calling Frank Patterson—especially since I gave my housekeeper time off from now until Christmas to get ready for her children's visit."

"I cooked breakfast." She pointed at the sink with the spatula and smiled. "I didn't say anything about washing dishes."

She stretched across the counter to pour him a mug of coffee. Her nightshirt rode up creamy thighs and Grant's gaze glued itself to the sight while his fingers itched to reach out and touch the soft skin. Would it be as smooth as he remembered? Would she shudder like she had that one fateful time he'd allowed himself to see her as a woman?

He bit back a curse. He wasn't about to give in to carnal urges where she was concerned again. Their friendship meant way too much to him. It meant more than any other relationship in his life, and he wasn't about to put it at risk for something as fundamental as sex.

"Don't you have some sweats or something to wear with that thing?" He grimaced at the question, hoping she didn't hear the tinge of desperation in his voice.

Zoe stopped stirring the coffee and gave him a quizzical glance. "Why? I'm not cold. Does my nightgown bother you?"

Nightgown? It looked more like a T-shirt to him. "Of course not. I just thought you might be cold."

She shrugged. "I'm not."

"Good." What else could he say? That the sight of her sexy legs had sent his male hormones raging?

She would run screaming from the kitchen. Or, worse, she would stay.

He'd call Frank right after breakfast.

The call started off fine, but took a dive like a 747 with engine trouble when Grant brought up the subject of Zoe staying at the Patterson place. Apparently Frank's wife and Eudora Givens were good friends, and Zoe's ex-landlady had already given her version of events. Frank wasn't about to cross his wife by letting Zoe and her "menagerie" as he called it, stay in their home.

Grant hung up and sat staring morosely at the phone. How was he going to help Zoe find a place if even Frank Patterson wouldn't let her stay in her old home?

Grant ran his fingers through his hair and rubbed the back of his neck. What was he going to do? Who would let Zoe and her pets move in?

No one. That was who. The only way she'd find a place to live would be to give up most of her animals. That was never going to happen. But…she could leave her pets in the barn with his livestock while she stayed at the Patterson place and looked for a new rental. Frank would not object to Zoe living there alone.

Now Grant just had to convince Zoe.

After returning from school, Zoe went straight to the barn. She wanted to check on Maurice. He was used to living in a chicken coop, so the barn should be an improvement. However, she didn't know how he'd respond to living with horses. They were so much bigger than him. He might be nervous. As it turned out, Maurice seemed perfectly content. He accepted Zoe's petting with an expression of goat disdain.

"I talked to Frank."

Zoe jumped at the sound of Grant's voice. She whirled to face him. "I didn't hear you come in."

He smiled. "You were busy."

Zoe gave a final pat to Maurice. "What did Frank say?"

"His wife is a good friend with Mrs. Givens."

Zoe couldn't say she was sorry. She'd prefer staying with Grant until after the holidays. After the visit from her parents. "And?"

"She won't let you and your pets stay."

Zoe shrugged. "Guess you're stuck with me for a while at least."

Grant smiled. "Not necessarily."

"What do you mean?"

"I'm a problem solver, remember? It's what I do. If I can figure out the logistics on shipping beef to Japan on a scale large enough to keep my investors happy, I can figure out the living arrangements for one small kindergarten teacher."

"Watch the size cracks," she warned teasingly, but she was nervous. He was a problem solver, and she could see her plans for handling her parents' upcoming visit with aplomb going up in smoke. "So, what is your solution?"

"You can stay at the Pattersons' and leave your pets here with me. When you find a place, you can take them with you." His cat-that-found-the-cream-pitcher grin said that he thought his idea had merit.

Zoe's stomach tightened in a knot. Her day had been emotionally wrenching enough. She'd forced herself to put an advertisement for Maurice, Bud and her bird in the local weekly paper, along with sending flyers offering the animals free of charge home with her students. The last thing she wanted to do was to leave all of her animals behind and go live in the sterility of a pet-free household at the Pattersons'.

"You have too many responsibilities already. I can't expect you to take care of my pets too. You're the one who said you didn't have time to take care of a hamster."

"I don't. My hands will take care of your pets, and the real problem was that I didn't *want* a hamster. I'm not the small pets type and you know it."

No, he was the tycoon type, with a strong attachment to the land.

"I feel responsible for you being evicted and I am doing my best for you now."

She didn't need that reminder of his guilt. She'd much rather think he was helping her because they were friends. She really wished he didn't want to get rid of her. "They'll miss me."

"You can visit, Zoe. You're not going to be living in another state. The Patterson place is only about ten minutes away. Besides, I'll help you find a place and you won't be separated all that long."

Zoe dug in her heels. "No."

Grant leaned over and petted Maurice. "Be reasonable, Zoe."

"No."

He straightened, and his conciliatory smile was gone. "You're an unmarried grade school teacher. Neither your principal nor the school board are going to think highly of you living with a man."

Grant had a point and he knew it. She did too, which was why she hadn't argued too fiercely with him the night before. "It isn't going to be that long. I'll explain to my principal about getting evicted. He'll understand."

Grant shook his head. "He might, but other people won't. Do you want everyone in town talking about you?"

Zoe laughed, but it was hollow. The specter of gossip was all too real. "I don't care what anyone who doesn't know me well enough to know better thinks," she said, with more rebellion than truth.

"What about your students' parents?"

Why was he pushing so hard? "What about them?"

"Don't play dense, Zoe. You don't want your children's parents to think you're living with some man."

"You aren't *some man*. You're my best friend," she muttered.

He smiled. "Yeah. And because I'm your best friend, I'm not going to let you ruin your life, *niña*. What do you say? Should I call Frank back? The sooner you get moved to his place the better."

Zoe could not stifle the twinge of pain that Grant's eagerness to get rid of her caused. It reminded her too much of her dad's attitude when he'd moved her mom to Arizona. "Will you ask him if I can bring Princess and Alexander?"

Grant smiled, obviously relieved. "Sure."

"Great. You'd better do it right away. You wouldn't want me to have to stick around any longer than absolutely necessary." She could not help the bitterness in her voice.

Turning on her heel, she headed out of the barn. Grant couldn't have made himself clearer if he had shouted through a megaphone. He did not want her around. She should have expected it. She'd worn out her welcome with her dad before she'd ever been born just by being a girl.

Grant snagged her coat and stopped her mid-step. "Hold it."

She refused to turn around.

"I'm not trying to get rid of you."

Zoe snorted in disbelief. *Right.*

"Okay, maybe I am. But it isn't because I don't want you around. Come on, *querida*. You know it's for the best; you're just too stubborn to admit it."

She heard his words. In one part of her mind they made sense, but they did nothing to dislodge the lump in her throat. She wasn't sure why she was feeling so emotional. Perhaps the words hurt so much because they were almost identical to the ones her dad had spoken when he'd told her he was selling the family ranch rather than let her oversee it.

Heck, Grant probably had some convoluted reason why his actions on *The Night* had been best for her too. She'd hurt then and she hurt now.

She shook her arm loose from his grip and headed up to the house. Her happy reserves were all used up and she was in no mood to discuss why it was better for her for Grant to kick her out too.

CHAPTER THREE

GRANT tapped his pen against the desktop. He'd been working the figures on their most recent Japanese export deal, but he couldn't concentrate. The image of Zoe's hurt expression when he'd convinced her to leave her animals on his ranch and move into the Pattersons' was burned into his brain.

It didn't help that she'd been avoiding him ever since. She'd been by to care for her animals twice yesterday. Both times she had made excuses not to stick around and talk. Not that he had time for it, but it bothered him that *she* didn't.

Which made him what? Contrary, if nothing else. He should be grateful she was avoiding him with the way his hormones had been behaving around her lately, but he wasn't.

He missed her.

She could be so damn stubborn sometimes. Like when her dad had sold the ranch. It had been the only move that made sense.

The Jensens had had Zoe late in life, when her dad had been in his early sixties already. He'd wanted to retire. His only son had died a year before Zoe had been born. With only a vegetarian daughter who would no more sell the cattle for beef than cut off her own right arm, he hadn't had anyone to leave in charge of the ranch—so he'd decided to sell.

He'd been doing Zoe a favor, and Grant still wasn't sure what she had been so upset about. Certain times of year, like during the stock sale, she'd been miserable living on the ranch. He'd tried to talk to her about it once, but she'd changed the subject. He hadn't pursued it, not wanting her to realize he'd been the one to encourage her dad to sell.

They argued about enough lately.

Mrs. Patterson needed to vacuum under the guest room bed. Zoe sneezed for what seemed like the hundredth time while she pleaded with her cat to come out. "Alexander, you can't stay under the bed while I'm at school. The litter box is in the bathroom, with Princess."

Zoe was afraid that was the problem. She had left the cats in the bathroom with the litter box the last two days while she went to school. Alexander had not liked the confinement. Smart enough to realize that today would require more of the same, he had run under the bed and wasn't coming out.

Zoe had already tried her most coaxing voice and offering kitty treats, but Alexander would have none of it. Darn it. She was going to be late for school if she didn't hurry.

"If you don't come out from under there, I'm giving Princess your play mouse."

Who said cats couldn't understand plain English? Alexander dashed from under the bed and made a beeline for the bedroom door. Zoe would have lost him if two male hands had not shot out to catch the desperate feline. Zoe saw fancy tooled Spanish cowboy boots from her vantage point under the bed. Grant.

She scooted out and lifted her gaze to him. He was wearing jeans and a flannel shirt under his coat. So today he was working the ranch with his hands. It surprised her he still did it. He was a man of contradictions. A smart business tycoon who could ride herd on a horse or fly a helicopter to do it equally as well.

And he looked equally yummy in both business and ranch attire, which was not a comforting thought in their current relationship.

Jumping to her feet, she dusted her hands off. "What are you doing here?"

"Bad morning?"

"Not if you discount that I woke up late, had to skip breakfast and my cat hid under the bed. Now, even without breakfast, most of my students are going to arrive before I do."

"I'm glad I came over, then."

"Why did you?" She smiled so he'd know she wasn't being snippy.

Her annoyance with him had worn out sometime after dinner last night. It wasn't his fault she was feeling so vulnerable since her dad had sold the ranch. It had been a final slap in the face. The ultimate confirmation that Zoe wasn't the son he'd wanted and hadn't made much of a daughter either.

"The roads are bad." He smiled that killer smile that had been doing strange things to her insides since she was sixteen. "I'm going to drive you to work."

She sighed with exasperation. "Grant, you may not realize this, but there are women all over the county who are driving themselves to work today. Some are driving busloads of children to school and even more are driving their own."

He shrugged. "Better get a move on. You're already late."

"You aren't going to listen to me about this, are you?"

"No."

"I could refuse to ride with you."

"I'd just follow you all the way into town. Why deny yourself my scintillating company?"

Why indeed? It was pretty sweet he wanted to drive her himself, considering that even if he was concerned he could have asked one of his hands to do the chore. "Fine. Put Alexander in the bathroom. Check their food and water too, please. I'm going to get myself something to eat on the way, since you'll be driving." Grant was not the only one who could give orders.

He tipped his Stetson. "Yes, ma'am."

The fake drawl shivered through her, doing things to her heart and her desire. She forced a casual smile and squeezed past him, her breath quickening as her breasts brushed against his arm. She rushed into the relative safety of the kitchen.

When they were in the truck, she started to peel the banana she'd grabbed along with a yogurt for her breakfast. "How are my pets?"

"You know they are fine. You just saw them yesterday afternoon. Snoopy is sleeping out in the barn, though. He prefers it."

Zoe felt a pang in her heart. Snoopy didn't belong being cooped up in an apartment. He was a ranch dog. Grant had offered the big German Shepherd a home when Zoe had moved from her parents' ranch, but she'd refused. Maybe selfishly. But Snoopy had been her dog since he was a pup and she couldn't let him go.

Considering the results of her calls on apartments the

day before, she might not have any choice. Sunshine Springs wasn't a big town, which was why the rich and famous seemed to like it so much as a getaway destination. It helped that it was close to the ski slopes on Mt. Bachelor as well. But rental space for year-round residents was limited, and the rates could be astronomical.

No one she'd spoken to, no matter what kind of rent they charged, had been willing to rent to someone with a large dog like her German Shepherd.

Grant frowned. "Your bird is one of the loudest, orneriest parrots I've ever seen."

"You get used to his singing after a while."

He slid her a disbelieving glance before focusing on the snow-covered road. "*Singing?* The bird squawks loud enough to wake the cows in the pasture."

"I'll have you know that my parrot is a highly intelligent bird. He even says my name."

"Zoe, that parrot does not talk."

"Sure he does. You just have to understand his dialect."

Grant snorted.

"What about Bud?"

"He rolls all over the house in his exercise ball. I think he likes the living room best. I'm really not into small pets, but I let him do the ball thing a couple of hours each night."

Zoe smiled. "Thank you. Just think of it as training for when you have kids and *they* have small pets."

"I'm not getting married anytime soon. Ergo…no kids."

A sudden image of a little boy with Grant's dark coloring swam into her mind, making her long for things she could never have with him. "Do you have to drive so slow? I'm already late for school."

"It's a good thing I stopped by this morning to drive you. You'd probably have ended up in a ditch, driving too fast."

Zoe did not appreciate his comment. "Listen, Grant, I drive myself to work every other day of the year and I do not end up in ditches."

"So, your guardian angels work overtime? I knew that the first day I met you."

"Then I guess I don't need you doing it too, do I?"

"Maybe you don't, but you're stuck with me." His set jaw let her know that he found her flippant answer annoying.

It amazed her how quickly small disagreements escalated into full-blown arguments with him lately. This time she was going to remain calm. She gave him a conciliatory smile. "I've noticed."

He didn't return her smile. In fact, his frown grew more intense. "I promised your parents I'd watch out for you when they moved and I will."

Just like that, her resolution to stay calm went up in smoke. "Don't let a promise to my parents stop you from finding someone else to tyrannize. They gave up on me a long time ago."

He swore.

The rest of the drive to town was mile after mile of charged silence.

She unbuckled the minute Grant pulled up in front of Sunshine Springs Elementary School. Pasting a fake smile on her face, she unlatched her door and hopped out. "You don't need to bother picking me up. I'll catch a ride with someone else."

His jaw could have been hewn from canyon rock. "I'll be here at three-fifteen."

"Fine." She forced herself not to slam the truck door.

Grant waited until she was safely on the sidewalk before backing up. He exited the parking lot at a much faster speed than he had driven into town.

Zoe swallowed her frustration and headed into the building. The last thing she needed to deal with a roomful of five-year-olds was a bad attitude.

When he pulled up in front of the school that afternoon, Grant half expected Zoe to be gone. She wasn't. She stood talking to a couple of other teachers in some flowy cotton thing that flirted in the wind, with her legs encased in tight leggings. Didn't she know any better than to wear stuff like that in this weather? And where was her coat? At least she was wearing a turtleneck under the flowy thing.

Wasn't that the tattoo man from the other evening? If she thought Grant would let Mr. Leather drive her home, she was in for a shock. No way was she going home on a Harley in these conditions.

Zoe looked up and met his eyes. Grant breathed a sigh of relief when she said goodbye to her friends and headed toward his truck. At least that was one battle they did not have to get into. Not like this morning. He still couldn't figure out what had offended her so much. Did it really bother her that he had wanted to drive her to school?

A small, still voice chided Grant. It hadn't been Zoe's response that had escalated their argument. It had been his own. He was edgy and he knew why. Her dad had called him the previous evening, after she had taken care of her animals and left. He and Mrs. Jensen weren't coming for Christmas.

They had been invited last minute to join a group of retirees on a cruise for the holidays. Heaven knew why they accepted, but they had. Zoe would be devastated. He had given the number for the Patterson place to Mr. Jensen, but the older man had asked Grant to relay the news—said they were too busy packing to make another phone call, which was a load of manure. The man just didn't want to have to deal with his daughter when he told her they weren't coming back for the holidays. He'd probably dealt with enough grief from his wife, but Mrs. Jensen was an old-fashioned woman. She might argue with her husband, but she wouldn't outright say no to him.

Grant could have refused to tell Zoe, but that would not have improved the situation. Mr. Jensen did not know how to talk to his daughter. He would hurt her with his prag-matic attitude. He might even go on about Zoe's pets and the new mess she'd gotten herself into because of them, as he had to Grant on the phone the previous evening.

Much better for Zoe if Grant were to break the news. First he would have to get her speaking to him again, though. He was going to have to apologize. The thought did not lighten his mood.

She opened the passenger door and climbed in, shiver-ing. "You're late."

"I got caught on a phone call to New York on the landline." If he'd been on his cell, he could have left on time.

She harrumphed like only Zoe could. He imagined her little kindergarteners knew just when they had upset Miss Jensen without her saying a word. She had a look when she was mad or disappointed that left no doubt how she felt.

"What were you doing talking to that joker?" He hadn't meant to ask, but now that he had Grant wanted an answer.

Zoe's head snapped toward him and she gasped. She turned back and looked out the front windshield. "I do not know to whom you are referring. None of my friends are jokers."

He ground his teeth. "The guy in all the leather."

"I told you, his name is Tyler."

"So, why were you talking to him?"

"I talk to lots of people, Grant. Do you expect me to keep a record and report back to you?"

"Of course not."

"Good, because I would have to disappoint you if you did."

He had not meant to get so off track. "Are you going out with him again?"

"That's none of your business."

"It sure as hell is. I promised your parents I'd watch out for you."

"So you said this morning."

Grant cleared his throat. The thermal shirt under his flannel suddenly felt like one too many layers. "About this morning…"

Zoe gave him a sideways glance. "Yes?"

"I'm sorry I came on so strong. I know you're a good driver and I should not have implied otherwise."

Zoe's tense stance deflated like a pierced balloon. "Thank you."

He nodded. "Do you forgive me?" He knew with Zoe that once she gave the words it would be a reality.

She knew it too. She inhaled, and then let out a long, protracted breath. "Yeah, I forgive you. Are you sorry for calling Tyler a joker too?"

Grant smiled. "Don't push it."

Zoe laughed. "He really is a nice guy."

Grant just snorted. He wasn't about to say something to start another fight with her.

"You'll be happy to know that he's going out with my friend Jenny now. She was the redhead talking to us when you drove up."

He liked hearing that, but wasn't it awfully damn fast? Less than a week ago Tyler had been going out with Zoe. "What happened with the two of you?" he couldn't help asking.

Zoe's laughter filled the cab with more warmth than the heated air blasting from the vents. "Nothing happened with the two of us. We were never more than friends. I wanted to fix him up with Jenny all along, but both of them were shy to begin with."

Grant could imagine Jenny being nervous about dating Tyler. Most women would be. "Uh…Zoe, there's something else I need to tell you."

"Another apology? I don't know if my heart can handle it."

"No. Your dad called last night."

"Really? Did you give him the Pattersons' number? I didn't hear the phone ring."

"I gave your dad the number, but he was real busy."

She couldn't quite hide her disappointment. "Oh."

"They got invited on a seniors' cruise for the holidays."

"That's wonderful." She smiled. "I'm glad they're settling in so well. I was a little worried about Mom. She's so shy around strangers. I'm sure it disappointed her to tell her new friends no. There will be other cruises, though."

Zoe's concern for her mom's feelings made the news that they weren't coming even more obscene in Grant's mind. "They didn't say no. Your parents aren't coming out for Christmas."

"What do you mean? Of course they are coming. We've

been planning the trip since before I visited them at Thanksgiving."

He reached across the seat and pressed his fingers around her arm. "They changed their minds."

"They changed their minds about spending Christmas with me?" She made it sound every bit as bad as it was.

"It's not the end of the world, Zoe. Just think, you get to avoid the yearly Christmas argument with your dad."

"We don't have those anymore." He grunted, and she said, "They aren't as bad as they used to be anyway."

"You won't be alone. My parents are still coming, and Mom's expecting your help with dinner." It was a small stretch of the truth, but he was sure that his stepmom should be expecting Zoe's help for dinner.

There had to be things besides the turkey that Zoe could help prepare. And since his stepmother would insist on doing all the cooking, so the foreman's wife could be with her family, his comment wasn't a real stretch at all.

Zoe did not answer.

Grant decided to change the subject. It wouldn't do Zoe any good to dwell on her strained relationship with her parents. "Do you want me to swing by the Patterson place, or take you to the Double C first?"

"Just drop me off at the Pattersons'. Your hands are doing a great job taking care of everyone. I'm sure Snoopy wishes he could live over there permanently. He was never meant to leave the ranch. I should have taken you up on your offer to give him a home a long time ago. I've been too stubborn."

Grant hated the dejected tone in her voice. "I thought maybe you would come over for dinner tonight. I won't even make you cook."

She smiled at him briefly, and then turned to look out the window. "No, thanks. I have work to do, and I don't want to leave the cats cooped up in the bathroom."

"We can stop and pick them up." He ignored her comment about having work to do, sure it was just an excuse.

Grant would not let Zoe get out of the truck when they arrived at the Pattersons'. "I'll just run in and get the cats."

Zoe watched him walk away and reminded herself that at least she had him. Although she had told him that morning that she did not need him, nothing could be further from the truth. For as long as she could remember, Grant and his folks had been filling an empty place in Zoe's heart left by her parents' disapproval. She should not be surprised that her mom and dad had opted to join their new friends on a cruise. They'd never made it a secret that she didn't live up to their expectations.

How could she? She wasn't the dead brother she'd never even known, who by all accounts had been the perfect rancher's son. She didn't think her dad had ever forgiven her for being born female, maybe even for being born at all after he'd lost his precious son.

Grant opened his door and a blast of cold air whooshed into the cab. She shivered while he tucked the cat carrier in the extension behind the main cab.

"If you thought Alexander was unhappy about spending time in the bathroom today, you should have seen him getting into the cat carrier."

Zoe grinned. "That bad, huh?"

"I just hope we can find him later, when it's time to bring you home."

"We've only got one more day of school, and then I'll be there and he can be out of the bathroom and roam free."

"Except when you're looking for a place."

She said nothing to this reminder of the monumental task before her.

Twenty minutes later, the fragrance of melted butter and popping corn filled the kitchen, and soon the subtle aroma of brewing coffee joined it. Grant had suggested watching a DVD when they arrived, and she'd accepted gratefully. She knew he had stuff to do—he always did—but somehow he also always managed to make time for her when she needed him.

Grant Cortez was a really special guy.

When the popcorn and coffee were done, they went together to the entertainment room. "Want to watch an *I Love Lucy* episode?" Grant asked, knowing the old black-and-white comedy was one of her favorite shows.

"Sure."

She sat down on the couch. He popped in the DVD, then turned around to sit down and hesitated. What was the matter with him?

She patted the seat beside her. "The popcorn is over here."

After another short hesitation, and an unreadable look, he sat down, leaving a few inches between them. She scooted over to sit up against his side and rest her head against his shoulder. It was how they always watched DVDs. Grant sighed and put his arm around her shoulders.

The image of Lucy trying to stuff chocolate candies into her already full cheeks faded as Zoe became intensely aware of Grant's arm where it touched her.

This kind of thing had been happening with increasing regularity over the past year, and Zoe had always forced herself to ignore it. She'd thought *The Night* had well and truly cured her of any lingering romantic feelings toward Grant, much less any lust for his hard-muscled body. She'd been wrong, as the past year had too frequently shown…at least about the lust part.

She couldn't believe that she still wanted him after the painful rejection he'd dealt her when she was nineteen.

She'd been home from college for the summer, and they'd spent tons of time together, like always. Only there had been something different about that summer. It had been as if Grant had finally woken up to the fact she was a woman. He'd taken her places he'd previously only taken dates, and she'd caught him looking at her, his blue eyes darkened with what she'd been sure was desire, on more than one occasion.

She'd realized he was the embodiment of every romantic fantasy she'd ever had or would have when she was sixteen. Only he'd been engaged and living the majority of the year on the east coast then.

He'd gone to college near his real mother, so he could get to know that side of his family. It hadn't worked out the way either he or his dad had hoped. Grant's grandfather had died his sophomore year of college and he'd left his grandson the majority of his wealth, making Grant's mother angry and driving another wedge between mother and son.

Grant had started dating "the witch" that same year, and they'd been engaged ten months later. The engagement had ended when Grant had agreed to return to Oregon to run the ranch, after his dad had told him he intended to move with Lottie to Portland and oversee his business interests there.

To give Roy Cortez credit, he had offered Grant three options: hire a foreman with full decision-making authority, sell the ranch that had been in their family for four generations, or come home and run it himself.

Considering the fact that Grant had planned to live and work on the east coast, it had come as quite a shock to most everyone when he had agreed to move home. Everyone except Zoe. She'd known he wouldn't leave the ranch's running to a foreman, and that he would never sell it. He was a business tycoon through and through, but he was also connected to the land in the same way his great-grandfather had been.

His fiancée hadn't liked it, and had given Grant back his ring. He'd started dating lots of different sophisticated women then. There were always plenty to choose from, both in the winter, when ski bunnies showed up, and the summer, when supermodels lazed by their swimming pools in barely-there bikinis.

Zoe had been sure he would never look at her that way. She was too smalltown, and not exactly centerfold material, with her petite frame and mousy brown hair. But she'd been wrong, at least for a little while, and it had all come to a head one night that summer, when one of their many playful arguments had turned into a wrestling match.

She'd found herself pinned beneath his hard body and his even harder erection. She could still remember the shock she'd felt as his hips had settled into hers, making her intimately aware for the first time of the effect she had on a male body. And not just any male body. That hardness had belonged to Grant.

He'd kissed her and it had been incredible. So incredible that she hadn't noticed him removing clothes until they'd both been naked from the waist up and his mouth had settled on one of her nipples. The pleasure had been so intense it had shocked her right out of her passionate haze and she'd panicked.

She'd never even been French kissed before. She hadn't wanted to experiment with anyone but Grant, and he hadn't been available. She had pleaded with him to let her go. She'd thrown her shirt on and run from the barn and from the feelings he'd evoked in her. Later, she'd wanted to kick herself for being such an idiot. She could have trusted Grant not to hurt her.

She'd loved him all her life, and if it wasn't him it would never be anyone. So she'd decided to give him her virginity. He'd been supposed to escort her to a town dance, and she'd planned to offer him both her love and her innocence that night. Her plans had ended in her private humiliation when a model from New York had convinced Grant to drop Zoe off at home before taking her for a nighttime flight in his private plane.

The only consolation she could take from that night was the fact that Grant had not known her plans, or of the love that had been burning inside her for most of her life.

She would never give him the opportunity to stomp on her heart that way again.

Even knowing that the friendship they shared was as close to intimacy as they should ever get, she still desired him—and now it was getting worse. Like that summer four years ago, she sensed that Grant had become aware of the air sizzling between them as well. His breathing had turned shallow and his heartbeat thundered in her ear.

Zoe pulled back and looked into his eyes. Their normal blue lights had darkened with unmistakable desire. Zoe's lips parted involuntarily. His gaze zeroed in on her mouth and it tingled as if he'd touched it. The sound of tinny laughter came from the TV screen, but he didn't look away from her mouth and she couldn't look away from him. In a gesture born of nervousness, she flicked her tongue out to wet her suddenly dry lips.

Grant made a growling sound deep in his throat.

"Grant?" Her head was screaming, *Not again*, but her body was refusing to listen as she leaned just one centimeter closer.

"This is not a good idea." He said the words even as he cupped the back of Zoe's head and pulled her forward to receive his kiss.

CHAPTER FOUR

THE feel of Grant's lips against hers was so overpowering Zoe almost forgot to respond. Her body knew what it wanted, however, and she found herself arched against him, kissing him back for all she was worth. Her hands dug into the flannel covering his chest and she tried to eat his lips. He groaned and dragged her onto his lap, deepening the kiss.

At the first touch of his tongue Zoe lost whatever sense of reality she'd had left. Her mouth opened and she invited him in with little flicks of her tongue against his. His mouth was hot, his taste utterly masculine. How had she gone so long, forgetting how this felt?

Grant's body shuddered under her, and Zoe felt more than just his hard thighs against her backside. A responding wetness warmed her inner thighs and she clamped them tightly together in an effort to assuage the ache in her most feminine place. She squirmed against him, exultant when he bucked under her.

She licked the salt and butter from the popcorn off his lips, tunneling her fingers into his hair, awed by the feel of its silkiness against her skin. His hands were locked on her hips and she desperately wanted to feel them move. Then they did. Right up her body to her breasts that longed for his touch.

He brushed her already erect nipples as they strained against her top. She wanted more. She wanted to rip off every layer of cloth between her burning skin and his hands, and she wanted those talented lips that were wreaking havoc with her mouth to do the same to the needy little buds jutting against his palms.

She rocked harder against him and he groaned deep in his throat. He bucked upward, pressing his hardened penis against the juncture of her thighs, and she almost came apart.

It was too much.

It was too wonderful.

It was over.

Grant had torn his mouth from hers and yanked his hands away from her breasts. She kept her eyes shut and waited for him to resume the kiss, to go on to something better.

Seconds moved in slow succession.

She opened her eyes and could have screamed at the look of horror on Grant's face. He stood abruptly and she fell on the floor, landing hard on her bottom.

So much for their first kiss in four years.

He moved to stand near the recliner.

Zoe climbed up off the floor. "Ouch." She rubbed her backside. "What was that for?"

Grant ran his fingers through his hair. "Sorry. I…"

She waited, but Grant never finished his sentence. He just stared at her, like she had grown a couple of antlers…or worse. Her body ached from wanting, not to mention her unceremonious trip to the floor. Grant's dismayed features were not helping.

"Stop looking like that. It was just a kiss."

"*Just a kiss?* Zoe, you're my best friend. A man does not kiss his best friend."

This was getting out of hand. "Grant, I don't know if you have noticed or not, but your best friend happens to be female. There is no cardinal rule against kissing me."

"*I* have a rule against it."

Had he written that rule before or after their hot and heavy session in his barn when she was nineteen? She felt her face crease in a frown. "Well, you broke it."

"I know."

He looked so genuinely dismayed that she fought with dual desires. One to comfort him and the other to smack him. What was his problem? Being his best friend, she decided on comfort and leaned forward to pat his arm. He jumped back.

She glared at him. "Stop acting like kissing me was tantamount to cattle rustling." *She* was the one with all the reasons to keep their relationship platonic. He'd walked away from their last encounter with mutual passion heart-whole.

She hadn't.

He frowned. "This is serious, *niña.*"

"I know." Seriously disturbing. She might not think getting involved with Grant was up there on the list of her one hundred most intelligent life choices, but she sure as certain didn't understand his melodramatic reaction. "Why do you have a rule against kissing me?"

He looked at her like she'd lost her mind.

"It's a reasonable question. I liked kissing you." She knew it couldn't go anywhere, but it wasn't exactly the crime of the century.

Grant glared at her. "Get over it. It won't happen again."

"*Get over it?* No wonder women break up with you by the truckload. If you treat them all like mass murderers for liking your kisses."

"Stop dramatizing. We have enough to worry about without you getting theatrical."

Her theatrical? She wasn't the one turning a simple kiss into a federal offense.

He folded his arms across his chest, his stance defensive. "For your information, the women I date rarely break it off with *me,* and I don't mind them liking my kisses."

Okay. He was mad. That was pretty obvious. And he looked pretty confused too, but the words still hurt.

"What's the matter with me?"

She had not meant to shout.

Grant winced, then rubbed the back of his neck.

"Stop doing that. You remind me of my dad," she accused, out of all patience.

"Good. That's good. Just remember, I'm a lot like your dad. You don't want to kiss me again."

Zoe pinched herself. It hurt. "Ouch."

Grant looked at her with that dumb cow stare that men got sometimes when faced with a *relationship* discussion. "Why did you do that?"

"I wanted to know if this was some bizarre dream. Unfortunately, it's not." She rubbed at her arm where she had pinched it. She could not understand Grant's reaction. She had a good reason for avoiding a relationship with him, but what was *his* problem with *her*?

She needed some time to think—away from the maddening man trying to convince her that he was just like her father. No two men could be more different. Grant had never made Zoe feel like she needed to be something or someone different to earn his approval. He'd hurt her when she was nineteen, but he hadn't known how much. After all, as far as he was concerned she was the one who had run from the barn.

He didn't know that she'd changed her mind and been prepared to take their relationship to a deeper level. But that didn't excuse him turning to another woman so quickly, or the fact he hadn't talked over what had happened with her before doing so. Zoe wasn't the only one who had seen her and Grant as a couple that summer.

"I'm going to check on Snoopy and Maurice."

"Great. I'll start dinner."

His obvious relief set her teeth on edge. "Fine."

She left, stopping briefly to don her coat. When she opened the door, cold air and flurries of snow blasted her. She made her way to the barn, glad for the guide rope Grant kept during the winter between the barn and the hacienda. Her hands were numb in no time, and she berated herself for forgetting her gloves. She pulled her hands inside the sleeves of her coat and used the ends like mittens, holding onto the rope through the down-filled cotton. When she finally reached the barn, she yanked open the door and rushed inside.

She pushed the door shut against the howling wind and swiftly falling snow. She leaned against it, trying to catch her breath. One of Grant's horses neighed. Zoe's head snapped up at the sound. Snoopy came bounding toward her, barking a greeting.

"Hush, dog." Zoe sank to her knees to hug him, and scratched him behind the ears. Snoopy crooned low in his throat at her affectionate scratching.

"Grant has a rule against kissing me. Can you believe it?" She patted Snoopy and stood up. She wanted to check on Maurice as well. "In fact, he would rather kiss just about anyone but me. He made that perfectly clear." She walked over to the goat's stall, talking to Snoopy all the way. "My best friend and self-proclaimed protector has a rule against kissing me. The man's got a screw loose. I never noticed it before. I'm not exactly a candidate for the lead role in *Fatal Attraction.*"

She entered Maurice's stall and leaned forward to pet the goat. He ignored her. Maurice had never really accepted Zoe. The only person he had ever shown any affection for was Mr. Givens. Zoe sighed. She checked Maurice's food supply and then left his stall.

Snoopy danced around her. "Well, screw loose or no screw loose, after that kiss I've got some thinking to do." Her body still tingled in places where he had touched her— even places he hadn't. The dog barked once loudly. Zoe smiled. "I'm glad to see you agree."

She sat down on the barn floor, glad for Grant's penchant for cleanliness and his ranch hands' follow-through. Snoopy nuzzled her neck before settling down beside her and laying his head in her lap. She scratched behind his ears again while she contemplated both her own and Grant's reaction to the kiss.

The one relationship in her life she knew she could count on was her friendship with Grant, and she didn't want to do anything to jeopardize it. She didn't want to get hurt again either.

It had been a whole lot easier when she'd been living in Portland and going to college, and then doing her teaching practice. Maybe coming home had been a mistake in more ways than one. She'd wanted to mend her relationship with her father, but that hadn't worked out. He'd sold the ranch and moved away.

Now, instead of being a blessing, like she'd thought it would be, her constant proximity to Grant was sending her libido out of control. While out of sight hadn't exactly been out of mind, without his constant physical presence she'd been able to convince herself that this passionate encounter in the barn had been an aberration and she didn't want him anymore.

Right.

Her body was still aching from a simple kiss. What would happen if they got even half of their clothes off, like they had that fateful night? And, more importantly, did she want to find out? Could she give him her body without giving him her heart, and if she did would it help her to dismiss this aching need pulsing through her once and for all?

She didn't know the answer to those questions, but she did know it irritated her that Grant had a rule against kissing her. It brought out a primitive, competitive side to her nature, and a speculative look settled on her face. It was a look that Grant knew well and one he'd learned to be very wary of.

The smile that tipped her lips was one that had sent him into damage control mode on more than one occasion too, but he wasn't there to see it now. Poor guy.

Grant could not believe that he had kissed Zoe. Talk about sheer male stupidity. Memories he'd fought hard to suppress rose to the surface, reminding him of how it felt to hold his best friend's delectable body in his arms. A nuclear meltdown would have been cooler.

After filling a pot with water, he placed it on the gas range to heat, and then moved to the fridge to pull out ingredients for the cheese sauce. He wasn't a fool, so why had he behaved like one? Zoe was his best friend. She was younger than him and needed to be protected, not seduced. He'd almost done that once when she was nineteen. He wouldn't have stopped, and he'd had her half-naked before she'd come to her senses and done so herself.

Letting her go had been one of the hardest things he'd ever done. It was right up there with trying to live with himself after seeing the look of horror on her face when she'd run from the barn after he'd all but taken her innocence. At twenty-four, he'd had a lot more experience than her, and she hadn't known what to do with the feelings their kisses had inspired but he had. And he'd tried to do it.

It was not a memory that made him feel good about himself. He'd moved fast to get their friendship back on track, and to do it had gone so far as to flirt with a woman from New York a few days later at the town dance. It had worked. Until now. He wasn't about to repeat his mistake of the past and risk losing Zoe's friendship, but, *damn*—she had tasted good.

Grant swore soundly. Remembering how good she tasted was not going to help him keep their friendship on the right footing. He didn't need to remember how good she'd felt in his arms either. She belonged to another part of his life. The permanent part.

Any physical relationship between them would have to be transitory. He didn't *do* permanent. He didn't even try to anymore. Besides, she would be no happier as a rancher's wife than she had as a rancher's daughter. And he'd learned that leaving the ranch was not an option for him. He belonged here. But she didn't. That left her place in Grant's life pretty well defined: friend.

And friendship was good, especially with Zoe. She didn't care about his money, his holdings, or his mother's connections on the east coast. Zoe only cared about Grant, and that kind of friendship wasn't something he'd ever willingly risk. Not even for soul-shattering sex.

He pulled out a block of Tillamook cheese and started grating it into a bowl.

"It's freezing out there."

He swung around to face her, still holding the cheese in one hand and the grater in the other. Snow stuck to her hair and jacket. Her hands were red from the cold. He wanted to grab her and take up where they had left off on the couch.

He yelled at her instead. "What the hell were you doing outside without gloves?"

She smiled teasingly. "Glad to see that you are in a better mood."

He ground his teeth together, in no mood for her joking. "I mean it, *niña.* If you had the common sense God gave a cat, you'd know this is not bare-headed and bare hands weather."

Her smile withered and died. "I was going to offer to help you with dinner—but without the common sense that God gave a cat I'm sure I'd do myself damage. And, since you persist in seeing me as a child, I can't imagine being of any real help to you either."

She turned around and left.

Had he offended her into going back to the Pattersons'? No, she would not do so without the cats. He continued grating cheese, listening for a cat's yowl or a door slamming, but heard neither.

She came back into the kitchen moments later, this time without her coat.

He stifled his relief and said nothing as she got herself a glass of water.

After a few minutes, Zoe's continued silence got to him. "Okay, I'm sorry." He hated apologizing. So why did he always end up saying he was sorry to Zoe?

."For what? Speaking the truth as you see it?"

"I do not think you are senseless and, while I use the term *niña* as an endearment, I do not think you are a child."

"Are you sure?"

"Positive."

She sighed. "All right, then. I forgive you."

Grant stifled a demand that she promise not to go outside without gloves again. He'd had enough arguing for one night.

She hopped out of her chair and started gathering the rest of the ingredients for dinner. The water came to a boil and he dumped the pasta in. "We'll have to wait until the snow lets up for me to drive you home."

Zoe's eyes widened. "You've got to be kidding. No way are you going to be able to drive me back tonight."

Was that why she had not stormed out? Because she thought she was stuck there? "My truck has four-wheel drive."

She stopped measuring ingredients into the saucepan on the stove. "Four-wheel drive won't do a thing for low visibility. It's a good thing we brought the cats with us."

Someone had sucked all the air out of the kitchen, and Grant regretted giving his foreman's wife time off for the holidays. At least if she were here to prepare dinner they would not be alone. "You can't spend the night."

"Don't be silly. Of course I can."

He was drowning. "You don't have any clothes with you."

She gave him a cheerful smile. "You can lend me something to sleep in."

Zoe sleeping in his clothes? The image of her wearing one of his T-shirts as a nightgown caused an uncomfortable sensation in his groin. A mental picture of her wearing *him* made his jeans feel like a pair of Speedos two sizes too small. "The snow will let up."

"I hope so." She tasted the cheese sauce by dipping her finger in a spoon of sauce and licking it off. Slowly.

He itched to copy the action, her finger in his mouth.

"I don't want to miss the last day of school tomorrow." She took another tortuous lick of the sauce, this time off the spoon.

He needed better ventilation in the kitchen. He could not get enough air.

She turned toward him and offered the spoon. "Want to try it? I think it's done."

"N-no." His voice hadn't cracked like that since middle school. He cleared his throat. "I trust you."

She shrugged. "You're missing something. It's really good." Then she proceeded to lick every last drop of melted cheese from the spoon.

The pasta boiled over and he jumped forward to save it. He grabbed the pot, inwardly cursing his earlier inability to look away from Zoe's tantalizing lips on the spoon. The noodles looked cooked. He tested one and burnt his tongue. "Ouch."

She handed him a glass of water. "Drink. It will help."

He grimaced, but didn't argue.

"You do this every time." She combined the noodles and sauce. "All you have to do is be a little more patient."

He did not interrupt her tirade. He was not about to explain that the image of her tongue on the spoon had all but robbed him of his senses. Hell. He had almost kissed her again. He tossed asparagus spears into a pan with butter and sautéed them.

They chatted about Zoe's class at school over dinner. The kids were involved in the Christmas program at the

Sunshine Springs Community Center the following week. "You'll go with me, won't you?"

He wanted to refuse, figuring that any time spent around her right now would just lead to further tortured urges, but he'd hurt her feelings enough for one day. "Sure."

"Thanks." She took a bite of her pasta and then licked the fork. The temperature in the kitchen shot up. "You know how nervous I get when my kids are performing, and I'm not even on the program committee this year."

"Yeah." He smiled, trying to hide his reaction to her innocent actions. "One year you'd unraveled an entire knit scarf by the end of the program."

She laughed, her head going back to expose the creamy column of her neck. He wanted to reach out and touch the smooth skin. This was nuts. He stood up.

"Where are you going?"

He stared. Where *was* he going? "The bathroom." What could she say about that?

When he got to the bathroom he turned on the cold water and bathed his face. Looking in the mirror, he glared at his reflection. "Knock it off. Zoe's off-limits."

The man staring back at him looked unconvinced. He splashed cold water on his face a second time and dried it. He felt marginally better. Now, if Zoe would just refrain from licking her fork, all would be well.

He went back into the kitchen and sat down across from her again. She smiled. He smiled back and nearly choked. She'd picked up a piece of asparagus and was systematically licking all the butter off the vegetable.

"This is really good. You sautéed these perfectly."

Her guileless comment mocked his randy response. He mentally chastised himself for his unruly thoughts, but it didn't make his jeans any more comfortable. By the time Zoe had finished the fifth prong of asparagus he was sweating and hard as a rock. At this rate he wouldn't be able to get up from the table when dinner was done.

She looked at him, her eyes darkened with concern. "Are you okay? You're perspiring. I hope you aren't coming down with something."

"It's too warm in here. I must have the thermostat set high." He knew it was a lie. He hadn't changed his thermostat in days. But what else could he say? Watching his best friend eat her dinner had him so hot he was melting?

He breathed a sigh of unfettered relief when Zoe did not take a second helping of vegetables.

Later, he got the longest T-shirt he could find for her to wear to bed and then headed for his office. Why bother going to bed? He wasn't going to get a wink of sleep, knowing Zoe's too tempting body was down the hall nestled in his old bed. She was going back to the Pattersons' tomorrow, even if he had to drive her in a blizzard.

Zoe snuggled down under the quilts on Grant's childhood bed. Dinner had been very entertaining. Grant might have a rule against kissing her, but he sure wanted to. His gaze had strayed to her lips twelve and a half times. She'd counted. One time he had only looked at her neck before looking away, thus the half. She was certain that he'd wanted to look at her lips.

She'd made it interesting for him, trying her best to eat her food as provocatively as she could. At one point, she'd almost felt sorry for him.

Almost.

He deserved it, making that crack about kissing anyone but her.

* * *

The following morning, Zoe woke up to chattering teeth and the smell of bacon cooking. It took her a moment to realize the person doing the chattering was herself.

Had they lost power last night in the storm? She could not believe that Grant or the foreman hadn't started the generator yet. She gritted her teeth and tossed back the covers. She yanked on the sweats Grant had lent her, which she had refused to wear to bed with the oversized T-shirt. She also donned a pair of thick socks, and went searching for a flannel shirt in Grant's closet.

After pulling on one of his shirts, that hung down to her knees, she went to the kitchen to find him. He stood at the stove, turning bacon. She wrinkled her nose at the smell of pork cooking and made a beeline for the coffee.

"It's freezing in here. Did something happen to the furnace?"

Grant slid a mug for her coffee across the counter toward her. "No."

"Then why is it so cold?" Zoe wrapped her hands around her mug, letting the heat seep into her chilled skin.

"Is it cold? Doesn't feel bad to me."

Grant wore a sage-green turtleneck under a black flannel shirt, faded jeans and cowboy boots. Of course he wasn't cold. The man was dressed to work outside. He did a lot more work on the ranch this time of year, so his hands had time to do the holiday thing with their families. But could he really be that dense? She walked into the hall and checked the thermostat.

"*Fifty-eight degrees?* Grant, are you nuts? No wonder I'm freezing."

She went stomping back in the kitchen and came to an abrupt halt at the look of satisfaction on Grant's face.

Evidently he had a few little surprises of his own. "This is about your kissing rule, isn't it?" *And dinner last night.*

If grown men could look as innocent as newborn babes, then he should have had a pacifier.

"Isn't it?"

He placed two plates on the table. One piled high with bacon, eggs, hash browns and apple slices. The other identical except, without the crispy strips of bacon. "Sit down and eat before the food gets cold."

She sat. "It can't get any colder than I am."

"Stop whining. If you don't eat and get a move on, you'll be late for the last day of school."

Her gaze skittered to the window. Bright sunlight reflected almost blindingly off the snow. "You're right."

She took a big bite of her hash browns and nearly spat them out. Groping for her coffee, she took a huge gulp, scalding her tongue in the process. She stood up, knocking her chair back, and weaved like a drunk toward the sink.

Grant looked up from his own rapidly disappearing breakfast and asked, "Are you okay? Something wrong with the food?"

Her hand gripping her throat, she choked out the word "water."

He jumped up and grabbed a glass from the cupboard. He filled it with water from the tap and handed it to her. She gulped it down and took several deep breaths before turning to face Grant. "What did you use to season the potatoes? Dried jabañero peppers?"

"A little of this, a little of that. You know I cook by the seat of my pants."

She wasn't buying it. Giving him a look that had sent

five-year-olds scampering for cover, Zoe advanced on Grant. "What did you put in my breakfast?"

He did not appear intimidated. "It's a little spicy, but you don't have time to savor your food this morning anyway."

"What does that have to do with…?" She let her voice trail off. Understanding came like air rushing from a balloon. "You didn't *want* me savoring my food?"

His cheeks took on a wind-burned look, although he had not yet been outside. "Like I said, you don't have time."

Right. It had nothing to do with his response to her and the asparagus the night before. "Whatever you say. Are the eggs similarly spiced?"

He shrugged.

Great.

Grabbing the apple slices from her plate, she carried them to the sink and rinsed them off. She was not taking any chances. She left the kitchen, munching on her apple, without another word.

CHAPTER FIVE

GRANT watched Zoe leave the kitchen and his appetite went with her. He'd woken that morning thinking she needed payback for dinner the night before. He'd worked out around two a.m. that there'd been nothing innocent in the way she'd eaten. He'd known her practically her whole life, and she did not eat that sensually.

He didn't know what had gotten her dander up—maybe the comment about him not minding other women liking his kisses—but whatever it had been, she'd set out to prove she could make him uncomfortable. And she'd succeeded. In spades. This morning it had been his turn, but now he felt like a skunk.

He picked up the plates and scraped the food into the garbage. Feeling guilty, he toasted her a bagel and slathered it with her favorite blackberry honey. He finished cleaning up the kitchen, washing the dishes. He had just rinsed the last plate when Zoe came storming in.

White terry cloth barely concealed the curves he had spent the entire night trying to forget. Her hair still had soap bubbles in it. Water trickled down her neck to disappear in the cleavage at the top of her towel. Grant thought seriously about opening a few windows. He needed air—cold air—and he needed it now.

Nothing competed with the expression in her eyes, though. He could see murder, mayhem and his own demise in her usually sweet-tempered eyes.

She slammed her hand down on the counter next to him. "So it's not enough that you set your thermostat to arctic temperatures and freeze me to death." She moved so close he could see the sudsy foam drying around her temples. "And then you spice my food with enough hot stuff to permanently maim my tastebuds."

She reached around him, but the sight of Zoe nearly naked had Grant paralyzed. If she was going for the cast-iron skillet, he was powerless to stop her. Her hand came back around and she waved a recently washed plate in his face.

"*This* is the last straw."

He stared down at the plate and could not fathom what had her so furious she would come storming out of the shower with soap still in her hair.

"I cannot believe you would stoop to washing the dishes while I was in the shower." She punctuated each word with a shove to his midsection with the offending plate.

Sudden comprehension made him smile. Big mistake.

"You think this is *funny?*" She nearly shrieked the words.

"Calm down. I forgot about the water-shower thing." The hacienda had had many updates over the years, but the interior plumbing had last been seen to before he was born.

"You expect me to believe that? You have lived in this house your whole life." She slammed the plate down on the counter with enough force that it should have broken. "First hot, then cold, then hot again. My skin is still trying to decide if you were attempting to scald me or freeze me to death."

Tears sprang to her eyes and she swiped at them. "Damn it, Grant. I was not the one who started the kissing last night. You broke your own rule, and taking it out on me is not going to make that fact go away. You don't have to torture me to within an inch of my life before I promise not to attack your manly virtue. I promise already."

With that she pivoted and headed out of the kitchen. She stopped at the doorway. Turning her head, she pinned him to the counter with her stare. "If you run so much as a teaspoon of water while I finish my shower, I'm feeding your favorite boots to Maurice."

He really had forgotten about the water thing. She was never going to believe him, though. She was right. *He* had started the kissing last night. She had responded with enough passion to keep him sleepless with longing for the next several nights, but she had *not* started it. However, he had not been the one to go all sexy in his eating habits.

She had to take responsibility for her actions. Well, actually, she had. So why did it bother him so much that she had promised to keep her hands off him? That was exactly what he wanted. Damn it. He needed to get his libido under control before he risked losing the one person in his life he would never willingly let go.

This morning hadn't been a good example of how to maintain friendship in the face of desire hot enough to melt rock.

What he needed was a diversion. Something or someone to keep his mind off of Zoe's delectable lips and even more delectable body. An image of Linda popped into his mind and he grimaced. Okay, so it hadn't worked with her, but he was a problem solver by nature. One small setback did not justify junking an entire strategy.

His mind skimmed through the possibilities and settled on Carlene Daniels, the bartender at the Dry Gulch. He played poker with the owner and a couple of local high rollers every few weeks, and she always served their table.

She had a sense of humor, and dressed like a walking commercial for prophylactics, but she didn't date much. She seemed to have a reputation, all the same, which was exactly what he wanted. A woman who knew the score and would help him get his desire for Zoe under control.

If he hadn't given his ranch hands so much time off he would have left on a business trip, but that wasn't an option right now. Which left Carlene.

Never one to wait when he'd decided to act, he grabbed the phone book to look up the woman's number. Zoe couldn't complain about him making a phone call while she showered.

Afternoon sun poured through the schoolroom window as Zoe picked up a bottle of white glue. She wiped the sticky mess around it with a damp paper towel. Her students had made Christmas decorations, and she had a mess of glitter, glue and little bits of colored paper to clean up. She didn't mind. She needed time to think.

Her anger toward Grant had finally cooled about the time her first class of kindergartners had gone out to meet the midmorning school bus. She could not maintain fury when surrounded by five-year-olds ex-cited about Christmas.

Breakfast had been a disaster. He had done everything possible to make her feel as welcome as a coyote at a roundup. Running the water while she'd been in the shower had been truly inspired. It was something almost as good as what *she* might have cooked up.

She bit her lip and swept some glitter off the table into the trashcan she carried. For as long as she could remember Grant had been the only person in her life to accept her unconditionally. When she'd become a vegetarian and her dad had gone through the roof, Grant had bought her *The Tofu Lover's Cookbook*. When her date had gotten sick the day of Senior Prom, Grant had taken her.

He had always been her knight in shining armor.

Remembering the hash browns that had about burned a hole in her tongue, she thought, *Some knight!* He'd gone from her hero to her sexual nemesis in the space of hours. Why was he so set on keeping their relationship platonic? He'd been every bit as involved in that kiss last night as she had.

And he wasn't exactly celibate. She didn't think he was a complete playboy. No one could afford to be in today's age. But he was experienced. Light-years ahead of her. If only he knew. She'd tried dating in college, and even gone so far as to go to bed with one of her dates. She'd been feeling like an anachronism, being a virgin at twenty, but it hadn't gone anywhere. She'd made a complete fool of herself, telling her boyfriend she just wasn't ready, getting dressed and going back to her dorm room.

He'd broken up with her a week later and she hadn't blamed him. She just could not imagine sharing her body so intimately with anyone but Grant, and if she didn't do something about it soon she was going to be the oldest living virgin in the United States. The more she thought about it, the more she was convinced that he would not have made such an all-fired effort to get rid of her this morning if last night hadn't affected him as strongly as it had her.

Scrubbing at a stubborn stain of dried glue, Zoe glared at the offending white blob. People had been saying she and

Grant should get together for years. Saying they were a natural couple. Even their parents got on that particular bandwagon once in a while. Of course her dad disagreed. Said Zoe had no business marrying a rancher with her affinity for animals.

It appeared that Grant took her dad's view. He acted like dating her would be tantamount to breaking the law. His law. Zoe wadded up the used paper towel and tossed it in the garbage. Well, she didn't want to date him either. She just wanted to have sex with him. Maybe then she could start looking at other men as something besides biological creatures that took up space on her planet.

She finished tidying up the classroom and headed to her car. She needed to pick the cats up from Grant's. Maybe she should offer to cook him supper tonight. No way was she letting him cook, but they had to eat.

She grinned, planning a meal that would make the asparagus spears look chaste.

Walking into Grant's kitchen half an hour later, the first thing Zoe noticed was a bouquet of roses on the counter. Her smile intensified and her heart started slamming against her ribs. Taking a deep breath, she inhaled the heady scent of the crimson blooms. He had not apologized this morning, but flowers were even better.

She plucked the card from the arrangement. It said "Carlene" on the tiny white envelope.

Carlene? Who in the world was she, and *why was Grant buying her flowers?* Hearing footsteps, Zoe hurriedly replaced the envelope among the scarlet roses. The jerk. He treated *her* like a pariah and bought flowers for some other woman.

She whirled around to confront Grant when he came in. She stopped dead, staring at the apparition before her. "Grant?"

"What?"

It *was* Grant. The voice was the same. The incredible blue eyes. The nose. The masculine jaw shaved smooth. The mouth. That darned sensual mouth. That was Grant's body encased in tight black jeans and a T-shirt. Those were Grant's chest muscles rippling under the knit fabric stretched taut across his rib cage.

She'd seen him dressed for the office, and wearing similar suits or smart Armani sweaters for dates with his usual glamorous women. She'd seen him dressed to work the ranch. But never before had she seen him dressed so provocatively sexy. He might be worth millions and own the ranch he worked, but right now he looked like a cowboy going out on a date. A very sexy, dangerous cowboy.

She swallowed.

He leaned against the wall, his arms crossed over his chest, the muscles rippling in his forearms. His dark brows rose. "What's the matter, Zoe? You look like you've been eating my hash browns again."

"Who's Carlene?" she forced out between stiff lips.

"My date."

"Your *date*?" Was that husky voice hers?

"Yeah." He even sounded like one of his cowboys. She wondered if his Spanish great-grandfather had been equally chameleon-like. The man had certainly made the Double C a solid going concern, through hard work and business acumen a lot like Grant's.

"As in for tonight?"

Grant gave her a look that said he thought she'd been sniffing glue instead of wiping it up. "Yeah."

There went her plans for another sexy dinner. Looking around the kitchen, she noticed other things besides the roses. Grant had set out silverware and plates on the counter to be carried into the dining room. "You're having your date *here*?"

"She wants to cook me dinner."

Carlene probably planned on serving him asparagus and a whole lot more. The hussy. "Are you sure that's a good idea?"

"Why not?" The sound of a bird screeching reached her ears. Grant frowned. "Is there any way to keep that parrot quiet tonight? He's going to ruin the mood."

Too bad. She did her best to look apologetic while silently praising her parrot for his screeching tenor. "I'm sorry. He's just like that. Nothing I can do."

"I'll think of something."

She just bet he would. "I guess I'll pick up the cats and get out of your way."

"Great."

It was a good thing Zoe didn't have a glass of water handy. Grant would be the only contestant in a wet T-shirt contest otherwise. "Right. Well. I'll just get the cats."

She found Alexander and Princess and put them in the cat carrier. Walking into the bedroom she had slept in the first night, she stopped to talk to Bud, the hamster. "Things are looking bleak, Bud. I've finally decided to stop pussy-footing around my feelings for Grant and he's got a date with another woman."

He ran on his little exercise wheel, ignoring her. Males.

Zoe wondered if Carlene liked rodents. She racked her brain, trying to remember if she had ever met the woman.

An image of deep cleavage and incredibly tight, short skirts rose in Zoe's mind. The weekend bartender at the Dry Gulch. The woman went through men faster than Grant went through relationships—or at least that was what people said.

Zoe wanted to scream. She smiled instead, and loosened the door on top of Bud's cage.

Whistling a Christmas carol, Zoe picked up the cat carrier and left. She didn't bother saying goodbye to Grant. She could do without another dose of his sexy, tight T-shirt.

Grant put the finishing touches on the table. The roses looked good. Romantic. So did the rest of the dining room, thanks to his mother's penchant for French provincial décor. She'd been gone for more than two decades, but because Lottie had only been interested in changing a few rooms of the ranch house, her influence remained.

The front doorbell rang and he rushed to answer it. When he opened the door, cold air and perfume assailed him. It wasn't an unpleasant scent, but it wasn't Zoe's either.

Which was the point, he reminded himself.

"Hi, Grant," Carlene said softly, smiling. Her dress wasn't nearly as revealing as the gear she wore to work in, but it accentuated her voluptuous curves all the same. "There's one more bag in the car if you'd like to get it."

"I'll get it. You go on in."

He moved back, but she still managed to brush his arm with her chest. He was surprised when she jumped and apologized. When he walked into the kitchen with the bags a minute later, he found her rummaging through the cupboards.

She smiled, her expression a cross between nervous and welcoming. "I was looking for a pot to boil the pasta."

"Over here." He pulled out the pot he had used to make dinner for Zoe the night before.

"Thanks."

"Sure."

She turned to the sink and started filling the pot with water. "Want to make the salad?"

"Okay."

She tossed him a bag of salad.

Zoe never bought premade salad. She said it was a drain on the environment's resources. And that was the last comparison he was going to make between his date and his best friend tonight. After rinsing the lettuce and tossing it in a bowl along with the pre-mixed dressing, Grant had to admit it sure was easier than cutting everything up.

"I'll have to make Zoe try this sometime. It's a snap." He grimaced, wishing he hadn't brought her up.

Carlene gave him an inquiring look. "Is she the schoolteacher? The one that dated Tyler?"

Grant frowned. "Yeah."

Carlene laughed. "I would never have picked those two for a couple. She treated Tyler nice, though. He was always going on about what a lady she is."

"That's Zoe."

"She even introduced him to his new girlfriend. Another teacher. I think Tyler's really in love."

The last thing Grant wanted to do was talk about Zoe, love and Tyler, the man in leather. "Want me to do anything else?"

"Sure, sugar," she said flirtatiously, her Texas accent drawing the words out. "Only it will have to wait until after dinner."

Maybe this whole date thing was not such a good idea after all. He wanted sex, but the knowledge that it wasn't going to be with Carlene hit him between the eyes with the force of a hammer. She was a lovely woman, but right now the only female who attracted him was Zoe.

So much for his great diversionary tactic.

"You can make dessert." She said it nervously, and he wondered why.

"Sure."

"I brought whipped cream, chocolate, and maraschino cherries."

"I don't have any ice cream."

Carlene winked at him, but her face looked like she'd just added a whole layer of blusher. "I'm sure we'll come up with something."

She moved forward almost awkwardly, her bee-stung lips parted for a kiss. Grant started backing away and she kept coming. The sound of an earsplitting screech came from down the hall.

Carlene jumped and let out a pretty good screech of her own. "What was that?"

"Zoe's bird."

"What is her bird doing here?"

Grant explained about Zoe getting evicted. He left out the part about Bud, not proud of the fact that he had been instrumental in getting his friend evicted from her apartment.

"That's a lot of pets for a single woman to have. No wonder she's having a hard time finding a new place. I wouldn't try to take care of so many, but I bet she never gets lonely," Carlene said wistfully.

Grant frowned, the comment about loneliness making him wonder for the first time if Zoe had so many pets for that very reason. "She just has a soft spot for animals."

"And then some."

"I better go check on the bird."

"All right."

As he walked down the hall toward the bedroom with the parrot, he wondered what in the hell he was supposed to do about Carlene's whipped cream and cherries. She acted like a woman ready for a night of no-strings sex, but it didn't ring true. Maybe Carlene was the lonely one. Whatever her motives, he wasn't making dessert with her, tonight or any other night.

And, damn it, he should have realized that before he ever asked her out. He kept telling himself he wasn't a stupid man, but he certainly gave a good imitation of one sometimes.

The sound of screaming from the kitchen interrupted his thoughts. Grant rushed back in the room without checking on the bird.

Carlene stood on a kitchen chair, yelling loud enough to be heard in the next county. When she saw Grant she launched herself at him, literally flying through the air. *"Mouse. It was a mouse."* She grabbed his shirtfront, shaking him. "He ran over my foot. He was brown and white and…" She trailed off with shuddering breaths.

A brown and white mouse? *Bud.* Grant pushed Carlene into a chair. "I'll get you a glass of water."

"Water?" She jumped up and started screaming again. *"There."* She pointed at the corner. *"He's over there."*

Grant made a dash for Bud, but the hamster scurried under the cabinets. Grant turned around. Carlene was no longer screaming, but she was back on top of the chair.

"It's okay. It's just Zoe's pet hamster."

She made an obvious bid for composure. "Your friend keeps rodents for pets?"

"Well, actually it was my hamster, and she agreed to

keep him for me." Grant got down on his knees and peered under the cabinet. "Do you mind helping me find him? He could get hurt, being out of his cage like this."

The look of horror that cast her features in stark relief could not be feigned. "I'd like to, I really would. I don't want him hurt, even if he is a…" She swallowed. "A rodent. But I can't. I'm sorry."

She sounded it too. She really was a nice woman, even if a little forward.

"It's all right. I'll find him on my own."

Grant heard her step down off the chair. "I think I'd better go."

Her turned toward Carlene, half of his attention still on the cupboard Bud had disappeared behind.

She was buttoning her coat. He jumped up. "Hey. I'll find the hamster. Relax."

She shook her head. "No, really… I don't think I was up to tonight anyway." Then she was out the door before he could answer.

What had she meant by that? *Damn.* Where was Bud?

CHAPTER SIX

"You lost Bud?"

How could he lose the hamster? Guilt settled in Zoe's stomach and made her defensive. "I cannot believe you let your date scream the place down and lost the hamster." She jumped out of bed, the phone still cradled to her ear. "I'm coming over."

It was not as if her idea to snuggle in bed watching old movies to keep her mind off Grant's date was working anyway. Images of Grant and Carlene had superimposed themselves over the people on the screen.

She arrived at the Double C to find all the lights in the house blazing. She knocked at the kitchen door, not wanting to give Bud a chance to escape when she opened it. Grant swung the door open almost immediately. His hair was disheveled. Had he been running his fingers through it in agitation, or had Carlene done it before leaving in a huff over the hamster?

Dislodging the torturous thought with effort, Zoe asked, "Have you found him yet?"

They *had* to find the little guy. Not only for Bud's sake, but also because she'd already promised one of her students he could have the hamster.

Grant ran his fingers through his hair and shook his head. "No. I found a space between one of the cabinets and the wall."

Zoe frowned. "You think he's in the wall?"

Grant nodded. "Yeah."

"I can't believe it." She groaned. "How are we going to get him out?"

Rubbing the back of his neck, Grant sighed. "I think we need to give it some time and some quiet. If I were a hamster, Carlene's screams would have made me go into hiding too."

Zoe fought to hide a smile. "I guess she doesn't like rodents, huh?"

"No. I don't think she likes me much anymore either."

Zoe could not lie and say she was sorry. She looked around the kitchen and took in the half-prepared dinner. "You didn't eat yet?"

He shook his head. "No." His stomach rumbled.

The poor guy was starving. Looking at the pasta draining in the strainer, and the half-prepared white sauce, Zoe figured she could finish dinner. She started pulling ingredients from the bags. "Run some hot water over the pasta to reheat it."

Grant nodded. He picked up a bowl of salad, the lettuce obviously wilted from sitting coated in dressing. "I guess this is a goner."

"Yeah." She peered into the bowl. "We'll have to have cooked vegetables."

"Okay. No asparagus, though. I'm, uh, not in the mood."

She turned her face to hide the grin his words provoked. "I saw a bag of California Blend in the freezer last night. Pull it out. We'll nuke it with a little butter and Parmesan."

She finished the white sauce, adding the canned salmon Carlene had left behind, while Grant reheated the pasta and cooked the vegetables. She made a mental note to drop off replacement ingredients with Carlene sometime the following week. Zoe hoped that would allay some of her current feelings of guilt. After all, she'd been responsible for ruining the date…and losing the hamster. She sighed and grabbed the last bag on the counter to empty its contents.

Suddenly Grant's hand shot in front of her and snatched the sack. "We don't need this stuff. It was for dessert."

Zoe made a grab for the brown paper. "Great. I deserve something sweet after cooking your dinner."

Grant did not release his hold on the bag. "Not this."

"Why not? Did Carlene buy some expensive dessert and you'll feel guilty eating it without her?"

He coughed. "Uh. No."

"Look, whatever it is, I'll replace it tomorrow. I'm in the mood for sugar." She yanked on the bag.

"No, Zoe." He yanked it back.

The paper tore. A spray can of whipped cream, a squeeze bottle of chocolate sauce and a small jar of maraschino cherries tumbled onto the counter between them. "Mmm. Looks good. What kind of ice cream did she bring to go with this?"

Grant did not answer. Zoe looked at him. He would not meet her eyes. Puzzled, she looked from him to the toppings and then back at him again. "Come on, Grant. What kind did she bring? Sinful Pleasures or something?"

"Look, let's just get dinner on the table. I'm starving."

Fine. She'd see for herself. Moving across the kitchen, she still could not fathom what had him so embarrassed. She opened the freezer door and rooted around inside. She closed it, and then turned to face Grant. "There isn't any ice cream."

Grant frowned. "I know."

"Did you forget to buy it?"

"No."

"What good are ice cream toppings without ice cream?"

Maybe that was why Grant had acted so strangely about her opening the bag. She looked back over to the counter at the toppings. Sudden understanding stabbed at her with the pain of a branding iron. "You. Planned. To. Have. Carlene. For. Dessert."

How could he do this? She knew Grant wasn't chaste, but *this*? To her knowledge he wasn't into one-night stands, and this was his first date with Carlene. He hadn't even slept with his last girlfriend. He'd be furious to find out that she knew, but women talked…just like men.

Zoe felt her throat clog with tears. She had to get out of there before she made an idiot of herself. She was definitely overreacting, but she couldn't seem to help it. She whipped around toward the door. "Leave a bowl of food out for Bud. He'll get hungry and come out."

She rushed into the mudroom and grabbed her coat. Jerking it on, she cursed her impulse to feed Grant. If she hadn't finished making dinner, she never would have known about his plans with Carlene and her heart would not be breaking in a million bitty pieces on the linoleum of the mudroom floor.

Just why her heart was involved at all was not something she wanted to dissect right now.

She did not make it three steps to the door. Grant spun her around, keeping a firm hold on her upper arms. "I did not plan anything. You know me better than that."

"I thought I did."

"You do, damn it."

She glared at him, her eyes blurred with tears she refused to shed. "Then what were you going to do with ice cream toppings? Eat them on top of crackers?"

"I was not going to do anything with them."

"You expect me to believe that?"

"It doesn't matter. Being my best friend does not give you the right to dictate how I handle my relationships."

The vise constricting her heart tightened until Zoe thought she could not breathe. "It's already a relationship? I thought this was your first date."

He sighed. "That's not the point."

Zoe shoved away from him, breaking his hold on her arms. "You're right. The point is that I need to leave. Who knows? Maybe you can still salvage your evening with Carlene. At her place."

She spun around. Checking to make sure Bud was not waiting to make a break for outside, she yanked open the door and rushed out. She could not get away from Grant fast enough. He called her name, but she ignored it. She had already made an utter fool of herself. She wasn't going back for more.

She barely remembered her drive back to the Pattersons'. Her mind was filled with Grant's words. She fought against the truth, but finally had to accept it. Being his best friend did *not* give her the right to judge his actions or his relationships.

It didn't give her the right to try to seduce him either. Even if he *was* the only man she could seriously contemplate making love to.

She let herself into the house and then let the cats out of

the bathroom. They followed her to the bedroom, obviously too sleepy to punish her for leaving them in the bathroom with their usual aloof behavior. She undressed. Climbing under the covers, she called the cats to her. Mercifully, they both came willingly and cuddled against her. She needed their warmth. She felt so cold inside. So lost.

Animals had always been safe. Safer than people. For as long as Zoe could remember she had trusted her animal friends to give her the unconditional acceptance she craved and did not receive from the people around her. Everyone but Grant. It hurt, but she had to face facts. If she insisted on crossing the line into intimacy, she could very well lose the one person she could not bear to do without.

"I made a big mistake." She stroked Alexander's silky fur. He began to purr, the soft sound vibrating through Zoe's fingertips. "I went ballistic on Grant over his plans with his date tonight. And it wasn't any of my business."

So much for her idea to satisfy her lust for Grant and keep her heart out of it. Her reaction tonight proved her heart was involved on some level, though she refused to even contemplate the prospect that she might still be in love with Grant.

No. She'd been jealous, but it was a sexual jealousy. That was all. Not love. Never again. No way.

She shifted so she could pet both Princess and Alexander as she thought about her time over at Grant's.

He had a rule against kissing her.

He'd wanted to have Carlène for dessert.

How could Zoe compete with a woman who spray-painted herself into her clothes? Even if she could compete physically, did she want to? She'd thought she did, but if her behavior tonight was an indication of how she might respond when the physical relationship ended, she knew she couldn't risk it.

Not when it meant risking her friendship with Grant.

She'd really messed up, and she was scared to death she was going to lose her best friend. Tears that she hated to shed in front of others trickled down Zoe's face.

Grant loved her like a sister, and if she was smart he always would. If she tried to force him into a relationship he did not want, she would lose him. The cold that had begun to dissipate rushed back with arctic force. She would not lose the only person in her life who accepted her for who she was.

First thing tomorrow, she'd call Grant and apologize. Then she'd start looking more seriously for a place to live. He was the very best friend she had in the world, and the time had come for her to start acting like it.

Grant scraped the last of the uneaten dinner in the garbage. Why had he let Zoe leave believing he'd wanted to play dessert games with Carlene? The look of disappointment on her face had slammed into him like a drunk on Saturday night at the Dry Gulch.

One thing he had always taken for granted was Zoe's admiration. He would never forget the heady sensation of her adoration that first time he had met her and rescued her pet cow from being sold for beef. It had not been long before he had gotten addicted to that adoring gaze, and darned if he would not do just about anything to see that look in Zoe's eyes.

What demon had prompted him to tell Zoe his personal life was none of her business? All he'd had to tell her was that the whole dessert thing had been Carlene's little surprise and he had not been interested. Instead, he had as much as told Zoe that he'd planned to follow through with it. Hell, he had even implied a relationship, when that was the last thing he wanted with Carlene—or any other woman for that matter.

He finished wiping the countertops and stove. The kitchen was back in order. If only the same were true for his life. He did not know what was going on with him and Zoe, but it was going to stop. He hated fighting with her.

He looked at the clock above the stove. It was only nine. Making a decision, he grabbed his jacket and car keys. He stopped briefly in the family room and selected a video. The entire evening did not have to be a waste.

A trip to the all-night donut shop in town and forty minutes later, he stood on the Pattersons' front porch steps. He rang the doorbell. The wind whipped against his hair and batted against his wool-lined denim jacket. She did not answer. Her truck was in the drive. He rang the bell again. No lights were visible from the front of the house. Maybe she was asleep.

He was about to turn around and leave, disappointment an almost palpable taste in his mouth, when the door opened. Zoe stared at him through the screen, making no attempt to unlatch the door.

He smiled at her. Lifting the orange and white bag in his hand, he said, "I'm here for a truce."

She pushed open the screen door and stepped back. He looked down at her and felt like swearing. Her eyes were rimmed in red, and telltale moisture still clung to her cheeks.

She had been crying and it was his fault. He dropped the pastry bag on the hall table. "Oh, Zoe." He gripped her arms and pulled her against his chest, sliding his hands to her back. She remained stiff against him, but he was grateful that she did not attempt to pull away. "I'm sorry, angel. I'm so sorry."

Sobs erupted against his chest. "It's my fault. What you do with your women is none of my business."

Hearing that statement did not make him feel better. Pulling away from Zoe, he forced her to meet his eyes. "I was not going to have dessert with Carlene."

If anything, her tears fell faster. "It doesn't matter. It's none of my business. I'm just your friend. You don't owe me any explanations." The words came stuttering out between hiccupping sobs.

Just a friend? When had Zoe been relegated to *just a friend* in his life? She was the one person he trusted above all others. Not able to stand the sight of her tears, he pulled her back against him. "*Querida*, please stop crying."

"I'm trying."

She took several deep breaths. He rubbed her back, attempting to comfort her. "You're the best friend I've ever had. I don't trust anyone like I trust you."

"That makes it worse," she wailed. She broke away from him and backed up until she met the wall. Narrow, the hallway only afforded a few feet of distance between them. "You trusted me and I ruined your date."

Feeling like he did not know the script, he demanded, "What are you talking about?"

"I left Bud's cage door open."

What? "Why?"

"Because I was jealous of Carlene."

"I can't believe this."

She looked miserable. "I know. It was a despicable thing to do, and now Bud's lost. He could be anywhere, freezing his little paws off."

More likely in Grant's walls somewhere, eating his wiring. "We'll find Bud. That's not what I was talking about. I can't believe you were jealous of Carlene. She's just a date. You are my best friend."

Zoe's eyes locked on to his. "Am I?"

Furious that she could doubt their long-standing bond, he stalked over to her. He stopped when his boots met her bare toes. Moving his face inches from hers, he spoke, shooting his words out like bullets. "You might drive me right up a wall with your melodrama. You might piss me off royally when you refuse to let me drive you to town. None of that changes the fact that you are one of the most important people in my life."

"Thank you." She gave a half-smile and wiped at the tears on her cheeks with her hands. "I think."

"For the record, I am not interested in playing dessert games with Carlene."

Zoe's smile blossomed to a grin. She looked down at the bag on the table. "Donuts?"

He returned her smile. "Yeah. Your favorite—toasted coconut." He pulled a video case from his coat pocket and waved it in the air. "Movie."

"The Quiet Man?"

He nodded. "Uh-huh."

"You really aren't mad at me about Bud?"

He shook his head. "Uh-uh."

"Okay." Zoe turned around and headed toward the back of the house.

Grant grabbed the donuts and followed her. When she passed the entrance to the living room, he stopped. "Where are you going?"

"To the bedroom. I moved the VCR in there earlier."

"I'll move it back to the living room for you."

"Why bother?" She turned around to face him, her tear-stained cheeks causing guilt to tug at him. "It's already set up. Why not just watch it in there?"

Because he did not want to torture himself. Not about to admit that to her, he shrugged. "Be more comfortable in the living room."

Shutters came down in her eyes. She nodded. "You're probably right. You set up the VCR while I put on some sweats."

He did not like the emotionless expression on her face, or the flat tenor to her voice. She was slipping away from him again, and that scared the hell out of him. "Forget it. We'll watch it in your room."

When she remained silent, he added, "If you fall asleep, I won't have so far to carry you."

She looked at him, serious as a heartbeat. "I won't fall asleep."

"I was just teasing."

Her smile looked forced. Damn, he had to get things back to normal with them. Taking long strides, he passed her by. Grabbing her wrist, he towed her behind him. "Come on, *niña*. You've got a date with the Duke."

He did not stop until he got to her bedroom. Doing his best to ignore the effect the sight of her rumpled sheets had on his libido, he tossed the donut bag on the bed. "You break out the donuts. I'll set up the video."

She laughed a Zoe laugh. A cascading breath of amusement, sweet with joy. His heart tripped at the sound and he thought the torture of watching a movie next to her tempting body would be worth that one giggle.

She dove onto the bed and whisked the covers over her

bare thighs. He nearly let out a sigh of relief when the supple limbs disappeared beneath the quilt. She opened the bag and pulled out two napkins, placing the pastries on them. He set up the video and then joined her on the bed, grateful for the covers between him and Zoe's enticing legs.

She snuggled next to him and munched on her donut. They watched the opening credits roll in silence. As the movie started he heard her say quietly, "Thank you."

He turned his head, but could only see the top of her hair. "For what?"

"Being my friend. I promise not to do anything else to jeopardize our friendship."

Something about the way she said it tugged at him. "You could feed my new ropers to Maurice and it would not jeopardize it. It might jeopardize your life, but not our friendship."

"My demise would seriously hamper our relationship."

So would throwing her on her back and making love to her enticing body. He forced down his raging desire and remembered that fact as she shifted to a more comfortable position next to him. It was going to be a very long movie.

Two hours of torture later, Grant was still castigating himself for choosing a video they both knew so well. It had done nothing to distract him from Zoe's proximity. Her laughter at the final scene choked off mid-giggle as she yawned hugely, covering her mouth with her hand.

She turned to face him. "You'd better head home. I need to get some sleep if I'm going to look for a place to live tomorrow."

"Got any leads?"

"No. Not many people want to rent to a zookeeper."

"You are not a zookeeper."

She yawned again. "Thanks."

He stood up and then walked over to the VCR. Popping out the video, he asked, "Why don't you just buy a house?"

Zoe looked at him, and unfathomable sadness settled in her eyes. He wished he understood it. What was making her so unhappy? "I told you, a teacher's salary does not stretch to a heavy mortgage."

"You know I'd help you."

She just looked at him.

"Okay, what about your parents? They'd help out with the down payment and you know it."

"The same parents who aren't coming home to spend Christmas with me?"

He felt the pain he saw in her eyes. "Yes."

"No."

"Why not?"

"Look, even if I wanted to buy a house, this is the worst time of year to find one. Even if I did find one, it would not close before the Pattersons return. I need a place to live *now*."

He knew she was right. "You could stay at my place until your house closed."

Zoe's eyes narrowed. "We've been through this. I seem to remember you saying something about unprecedented damage to my reputation."

He grew uncomfortable under her pointed gaze. "I'm sure we could think of something."

"Something like an apartment complex that allows animals?"

He picked up the now empty pastry bag and wadded it up. He tossed it in the garbage and then turned to face her again. "I'll let you get your beauty rest, then."

She nodded, clearly ready to do just that.

He stopped at the door. "I could take you. I need to go into town tomorrow and apologize to Carlene anyway."

She pondered the question a lot longer than he'd expected. He wanted to demand what was taking her so long to decide if she wanted his company, but something held him back.

"I guess that would be okay. If you are sure you want to."

Stung by her lackluster attitude toward spending time with him, his response came out more sharply than he'd intended. "Don't sound so happy to have my company."

She smiled sleepily at him. "Go home. You're tired and cranky."

She was probably right. What else would explain his current bad mood? "I'm going. What time do you want me to pick you up?"

She looked at the clock on the VCR and then back at him. "Not too early."

"Fine. You going to come lock the door behind me?"

She groaned, but got out of bed. He wished he had not said anything. Her oversized sleepshirt draped off nipples that had hardened when she'd slipped out from the warm cocoon of blankets. He could not drag his eyes away from the sight of the hard nubs pressing against the stretchy fabric.

His hand itched to reach out and brush first one and then the other. Then he would cup the fullness around them and caress it until she moaned like she had on his couch and rubbed her delectable body against his. He would then slide his hands down to caress the smooth skin below the hemline of her shirt, letting his fingertips glide under to touch the fleshy curve of her behind. His breathing grew ragged and he felt his penis pressing against the buttons of his fly.

"Grant?"

He shifted his unfocused gaze to her face and tried to make out her expression through the passionate haze blurring his vision. "Huh?"

"Are you okay?"

The genuine concern in her voice snapped him into focus. What the hell was he thinking? He took a deep breath and let it out slowly. "Yeah. Just tired, I guess."

She cocked her head to one side and looked at him. "Are you sure?"

He kept his eyes firmly on her face. "Yeah."

He turned and headed for the front door. She followed him, her bare feet slapping against the ceramic tile of the hall.

They said goodnight at the door, and it took more self-discipline than getting out of bed at the crack of dawn to muck stalls not to kiss her soft lips before he turned to leave.

CHAPTER SEVEN

ZOE stumbled into the kitchen, only half awake. Staying up watching *The Quiet Man* with Grant might not have been the smartest thing to do last night.

She hated apartment-hunting. Grant was right. She needed to buy a house. It was ridiculous to hold onto the belief that buying a house was something you did after you were married and had started talking about having a family.

Even if she found homes for all her pets, like she had for Bud, she knew it wouldn't take long to get herself back into the same predicament. She had no desire to live alone, and didn't like being limited on the number and type of animals she kept.

She slumped in the kitchen chair. She had been saving for a trip to Europe since her first paycheck. Her dad would say that was impractical. Maybe it *was* time to earmark that money for something more lasting and practical.

Something like a place to live.

Even with her savings, she didn't have enough for a decent down payment. But Grant had been right about something else too. Her parents *would* help her. If she asked. That was a bridge she'd have to cross later. She still needed to find a rental. It would take a miracle to find a house to buy, close on it and move in before the Pattersons returned.

She stood up, fumbled for the coffeepot and then filled it in the sink. Opening the canister of coffee she had brought with her, her nose perked at the vanilla nut aroma. Princess and Alexander rubbed against her legs.

She couldn't imagine life without her cats. "Morning, guys. Want some coffee? No? You don't know what you're missing." Zoe turned on the coffeepot. The sound of water filling the filter chamber lifted her spirits.

She opened a can of cat food and split it between Princess and Alexander's dishes. "How about breakfast?"

The cats walked regally to their dishes and sniffed delicately at the food before condescending to eat. Zoe smiled. "One of these days I'm going to give you some off-brand cat food and watch in glee when you eat it without being able to tell the difference."

Her pets ignored the empty threat.

She poured herself a cup of coffee, feeling decadent when she added flavored creamer. She took a sip, and savored the sweet concoction as its warmth slid over her tongue. Sighing with pleasure, she locked both hands around the steaming mug. Taking a few more sips, she gradually woke up.

Time to get a move on. She pulled the newspaper she had brought from town out of her book bag. Spreading it over the table, she searched for the rental ads. After circling as many likely possibilities as she could find, she started calling.

Twenty minutes later, she groaned in frustration as she crossed off the fifth ad in a row. No pets. *Someone* in this community must allow pets.

She needed a break. Time to shower and dress.

The hot spray felt heavenly against her body. She

stood for several minutes, relaxing under the jets of water. She lathered her hair, enjoying the floral scent of her shampoo.

The sound of pounding penetrated her consciousness.

Someone was at the door. *Grant.*

Muttering an expletive that would have gotten her mouth washed out with soap as a child, she stepped out of the shower. She grabbed a bath towel and wrapped herself in it. Rushing to the door, she cursed Grant's lousy timing.

The doorbell rang, and Zoe frowned. "Hold on. I'll be there in a minute."

Why was he being so impatient? It had to be pretty obvious she had not gone anywhere. Her truck was still outside. Flinging open the door, she said, "Jeesh. You didn't need to pound the door down. I was in the sho…"

Her words trailed off when she realized that it was not Grant standing on the doorstep, but Tyler.

"Zoe, am I glad you are here. I need your help."

Apparently oblivious to her state of undress, he shouldered past her into the kitchen. "Jenny isn't speaking to me. You've got to fix it." He sat down heavily in one of the kitchen chairs and dropped his head into his hands. "I don't know what I'll do if she breaks up with me."

Zoe edged toward the hallway, tightening the towel around her. "I'll get dressed and then we'll talk."

His head came up, his gray eyes looking right through her. "You've got to help me, Zoe. Jenny's one of your friends and you introduced us."

And that made her responsible for the health of their relationship? Evidently to Tyler it did. She sighed. Seeing Tyler's tough-guy-in-leather persona dropped completely to reveal his vulnerability tugged at her heartstrings.

She edged one more step toward the hall. "I'll help you. Don't worry. Just let me get dressed."

Tyler nodded. "Is that coffee I smell? I could really use a cup. I didn't sleep at all last night."

"Sure, the mugs are in the cupboard to the left of the sink. Help yourself."

"Thanks." He stood up and took a step, then stopped in the middle of the kitchen. His big shoulders started to shake. "I really love her."

Zoe's heart melted. She stepped forward and tugged Tyler back into his chair. Patting his shoulder, she said, "I know. It's going to be all right. She cares about you too."

Tyler used his fists to wipe the tears from his scruffy cheeks. "You think so?"

Remembering Jenny's rapturous listing of Tyler's attributes in the teacher's lounge that week, Zoe smiled. "I know so."

"Thanks." He put his beefy arm around her and gave Zoe a rough hug. "You're a good friend to have, Zoe."

Using one hand to keep her towel firmly in place, Zoe put the other one around Tyler and hugged him back.

"What the hell is going on?"

Zoe jumped back from Tyler at the sound of Grant's angry voice. Unfortunately, Tyler still had a grip on her, and her towel stayed with him. She screeched.

Grant bellowed.

Tyler looked past Zoe's now naked body and said, "Hi, Jenny. What are you doing here?"

"I don't know. I came to talk to my friend. At least I thought she was my friend. I did *not* expect to find her naked with you in the kitchen."

Jenny spun around and ran out the door.

Tyler chased after Jenny, Zoe's towel still dangling from his hand.

Zoe stood rooted. Shock warred with embarrassment at her predicament. Grant yanked the floral print tablecloth off the table and wrapped it around her shoulders.

"Get dressed." He glared at her. "You can explain when you are decently covered."

Still shocked from the unbelievable string of events in the kitchen, she did not register his words at first. She had returned to the bathroom, shut the door and dropped the tablecloth in a pile of purple pansies on the floor before she fully comprehended Grant's imperious demand.

She did not owe him an explanation. Grant was her friend, not her lover. Hadn't they established that yesterday?

Besides, it should have been obvious that she was not trying to seduce Tyler. The man was a basket case, and had taken off after Jenny without even a glimpse at Zoe's naked body. If the facts did not speak for themselves, there was not much she could add to them. Jenny was another matter entirely. Zoe would have to explain everything to her friend and hope Jenny was rational enough to believe her.

If only Tyler had let her get dressed when he'd first got there. But in his misery he had been oblivious to her scanty covering. *Men.*

Feeling annoyed at men in general and Grant in particular, Zoe stepped back into the shower. In her pique, she refused to rush herself. Grant could just wait for her, and for any explanations she might deign to give him.

Half an hour later, Zoe reentered the kitchen. This time she was fully clothed, in a pair of comfy cotton pants she had batiked the year before, a matching mock turtleneck and an oversized sweatshirt from her alma mater. Her tennis shoes squeaked as they hit puddles of water left from her dripping body earlier.

Grant sat at the kitchen table, a mug in his hand. The set of his shoulders and his thin lips let her know that he had not gotten over his initial reaction to finding her in the kitchen with Tyler. She frowned at him, letting *him* know she did not appreciate his attitude.

She walked by him and grabbed a paper towel from the counter. Going back to the puddles of water on the floor, she knelt down and wiped them dry. "You can stop glaring at me. Tyler and I were not in the middle of some hot and heavy loveplay when you got here."

Grant's chair scraped the linoleum as he pushed away from the table. "You could have fooled me. You were wearing nothing but a towel and Tyler when I walked in."

Zoe looked up to meet Grant's gaze. Mistake. His eyes were filled with fury and he loomed over her like an avenging angel. Trying to scoot back and gain some distance, she lost her balance and fell back onto her bottom with a plop. "Correction. I was wearing the towel and hugging Tyler. He needed comfort."

"If you comfort every guy who needs it with your naked body, I'm surprised your reputation isn't already shredded."

Putting her hands beside her and her feet under her, she pushed up from the floor. She landed two inches from Grant's chest. She met his eyes unflinchingly, giving him glare for glare. "That was a rotten thing to say."

She was so close she could see his nostrils dilate, a sure sign that Grant was furious. Zoe prepared for a rip-roaring argument with him. Instead he wrapped his arms around her, settling one hand on the small of her back and the other behind her head. Yanking her forward, he lowered his head and stopped.

Zoe felt like a deer caught in her daddy's headlights. She knew this meant danger, but she was too shocked to move. "Grant, I don't think—"

His mouth cut off the rest of her words. His lips were warm and she could taste coffee on his tongue. The tongue he roughly plunged into her mouth, still open to finish her statement. It felt good. He tasted wonderful.

Using the hand on the small of her back, he pulled her body into alignment with his. Electric shocks sizzled along her front where her legs, pelvis and breasts made contact with the hard contours of Grant's body. Of their own volition her arms lifted, and she locked her hands behind his neck.

The bones in her legs turned to warm candle wax and would not hold her up. They didn't need to. His mouth was no more possessive than his hands. He held her against him like a vise.

In the back of Zoe's mind, she knew this would not last. Anger had prompted Grant to do something he had made it very clear he did not want to do. Kiss her. She already felt the pain of his withdrawal, although it had not happened yet.

Refusing to give in to it, she determined to enjoy the sensation of being in his arms while it lasted. Relaxing against him, she gloried in the feel of his tongue branding her mouth, his hands holding her so strongly. She moved her lips under his, exulting in the groan that issued from him. He lowered his hand and cupped her bottom.

She could no more stop herself from rocking her pelvis against him than she could hold her breath under water indefinitely. She needed this. Too much.

He responded to her movements by backing her against the counter. He lowered his other hand to her bottom and lifted her until she sat on the very edge of the counter, her thighs open and Grant between them.

He didn't waste any time getting as close as he could get with only the layers of clothes separating them. He pressed his hardened shaft against the juncture of her thighs, and with only a small wiggle of her backside he was hitting her where it counted most.

She moaned at the feelings that rocketed through her at the contact. She wanted to be naked, with him buried deep inside her.

He squeezed her breast. She could not get enough air. Twisting her mouth from his, Zoe gulped in necessary oxygen. Grant moved his mouth to her ear and pressed wet, breathy kisses against it. Zoe felt herself spiraling out of control. She had never responded this way before, and if she didn't know better she would think she was about to climax.

He spoke into her ear. Whispering encouragement. "That's right, *querida*. Let go."

He thrust hard and fast against her. She ground herself against him.

"Yes." He yanked her shirt out of her pants. The first touch of his fingers against the naked, heated flesh of her stomach made her suck in her breath.

He moved his hand up under her shirt until he met her bra. Finding the front clasp, he undid it with a minimal amount of fumbling. She arched against his palm. When his thumb and forefinger closed over one nipple, she went rigid. He pulled and squeezed, moving his lips back to cover hers. His tongue plunged inside again. This time she met it with her own, thrusting her tongue against his in a dance as old as time.

The shudders took her by surprise. She yanked her head away from his and screamed. *"Grant—"*

"See, Jenny, I told you I didn't have anything going with Zoe. You think she would be making it with Grant on the kitchen counter if she was interested in me?"

A woman should *not* have to deal with this after her first ever orgasm in the kitchen. Between the look of abject horror on Grant's face and the glee on Tyler's, Zoe felt like punching someone. Jenny was giving her a look of wary hope, her freckled face streaked with tears and her red hair in a wild cloud around her head. Zoe decided that as a fellow woman and friend she could not disappoint her.

Grant pulled his hand out from under Zoe's shirt as if he'd just realized where it was. He would have stepped away, but Zoe hooked her arm around his neck and pulled. He was not going anywhere. "That's right."

Jenny swallowed. Even though she had not done anything wrong with Tyler, Zoe felt guilty when her friend scrubbed at her cheeks. "Then why were you naked and hugging my Tyler?"

Grant tried to pull away again, but Zoe held on. She whispered in his ear. "Work with me here. You owe it to me for the crack about sleeping around."

He stopped straining against her hold. Zoe let go of him and pushed until she had enough room to slip off the counter. Taking Grant by the hand, she led him to the table. "Sit."

He sat.

She patted his cheek and smiled. She turned back to Jenny and Tyler. "Do you two want some coffee?"

Tyler looked at Jenny for her answer. She shrugged. He said, "Yeah. That would be good."

"Fine. Sit down, and I'll explain how you found me hugging your Tyler wearing nothing but a towel."

Jenny frowned, but she sat down. Turning toward the coffeemaker, Zoe felt her still swollen nipples rub against the fabric of her shirt. Embarrassment swept through her. Changing her mind about pouring the coffee, she headed toward the hallway. "Grant, you get the coffee. I'll be right back."

Tyler asked, "Where is she going?"

"Don't be an idiot. What do you think we walked in on? I think she wants to put herself back together," Jenny replied.

"Oh."

Her cheeks hot enough to fry eggs, Zoe headed for the bathroom. She felt a little guilty about leaving Grant to face Jenny and Tyler alone, but not too guilty. He deserved *something* for that stupid look of horror on his face after the most beautiful experience of her life. Taking her to new sensual heights aside, Grant had clearly not changed his mind about his rule. He still didn't want to kiss her.

Well, this time he had done a whole lot more, and she was not sure she would ever get over it. Sighing, she looked in the mirror over the sink.

Her pupils were still dilated with passion and her mouth looked thoroughly kissed. Running cold water over a washcloth, Zoe let the liquid cool the heated skin on her hands and wrists. She bathed her face and smoothed the tendrils of hair that had escaped from her French braid. She refastened her bra and tucked her shirt back into her pants.

There was not much else she could do, unless she wanted to take another shower and change her clothes. She didn't. She wanted to get the discussion with Jenny over and start looking for apartments. Preferably without another all-out confrontation with Grant.

Coming back into the kitchen, she noticed that Grant and Jenny were both glaring at Tyler, and that Tyler looked like a man waiting for the executioner. Zoe's patience snapped.

"You can both wipe that look of nasty displeasure right off your face. Tyler has not done anything wrong, and I'm in no mood to deal with assumptions."

Tyler turned a grateful smile on her and Jenny's soft brown eyes widened at her tone. Zoe nodded. "I mean it. You want the truth, or not?"

Jenny looked at Tyler, then at Zoe. "I want the truth."

"Me too."

Zoe ignored Grant. She sat down at the table and looked her fellow teacher square in the eye. "Fine. I was taking a shower this morning when I heard someone pounding on the door. I thought it was Grant, because he was supposed to come over and go apartment-hunting with me. You with me so far?"

Jenny nodded.

"Good." She took a deep breath. "As you know, it was not Grant. It was Tyler. And to be honest I don't think he even noticed I was wearing only a towel and still wet from the shower."

"I *told* you," Tyler said.

"He was really upset. I guess you two had a fight?"

Jenny nodded.

"Well, he was beside himself at the thought of losing you, and he came over to beg me to talk to you."

"I couldn't stand to lose you, Jenny. I love you."

Hearing Tyler's declaration did nothing for Zoe's mood. She gave him an impatient stare and went on. "He hugged me when I promised to help him, and that's when you and Grant walked in."

Jenny's shoulders slumped. "I guess I owe you an apology."

Zoe shrugged. "Just talk it out with Tyler."

"I will." Jenny stood. "Come on, Tyler. We need to talk."

Tyler jumped up like a well-trained pup, which was pretty amusing considering how big he was. His look of eagerness resembled a pet as well. Jenny stopped at the door. "I am sorry I jumped to conclusions."

Zoe did not want to know. "I forgive you."

They left. She stood up, grabbed the coffee mugs and carried them to the sink. "You ready to go apartment-hunting?"

"Don't you think we should talk first?" Grant spoke from right behind her. She had not heard him move. How strange.

"About what?"

"A couple of things come to mind. The first being, why didn't you just go get dressed when Tyler got here?"

She lost it at the residual anger she heard in Grant's voice. "Because I *like* entertaining men wearing nothing but a towel. Why do you think?" She turned around and brushed past Grant. "Maybe you should go do your Carlene thing, and I'll search for apartments by myself."

"Forget it. We're going to discuss what happened here."

She spun around to face him. "I'm through discussing Tyler. Either you believe the worst of me or you trust me. It's your choice."

As she said the words, she realized that she owed Grant the same consideration with Carlene.

"I'm not talking about Tyler."

She sighed. The big confrontation. "Do we have to

discuss the other? I already know you've got a rule against kissing me. I figure you've got one against what happened to me on the counter as well." She looked at him. "Can't we just leave it at that?"

Grant's frown speared her. "At what? At the place where we both realize that I should not be kissing you but I keep doing it?"

"Uh, I think we did more than kiss. Well, I did anyway."

He ran his fingers through his hair. "I know."

"I'm sorry you didn't. Is that what's bothering you?" Men could get really cranky when they were left hanging, or so she had been told.

The look of horror was back. *"No."*

"I'm losing my patience here. There isn't anything we can do about what happened. Like I said, I know you did not want to do it. For some reason neither of us understands you have kissed me twice in the last week although you are firmly against the idea."

He sat down in the chair and dropped his head in his hands. He looked so much like Tyler had earlier that Zoe laughed.

His head snapped up. "It's not funny, damn it."

She stifled her giggles. "I know."

He fisted his hands against his legs. "We've got to do something about this attraction between us."

He had already ruled out the most logical course of action—giving in to it. "Like what?"

"Maybe we shouldn't spend so much time together for now."

Fear clawed at her insides. Was he saying that he wanted to end their friendship? He couldn't be. He had promised last night that he would not give up on their relationship even if she fed his boots to the goat.

"Please clarify."

He smiled. It was strained, but nevertheless a smile. "Sometimes you sound like a college professor, not a kindergarten teacher."

So? She'd talk like a blithering idiot if he would just explain what he meant by not spending time together. "Do you mean like not going with me to look for apartments, or not spending Christmas together, or what?"

He frowned. "I promised to take you looking for a place to live and I will."

"Okay."

"As for Christmas—we've spent every Christmas together since I was eleven years old. I'm not about to stop now. Besides, I like being in the good graces of my folks."

Relief seeped into her in tiny increments. "What exactly are you saying, then?"

"I don't know." He shook his head. "No more time together on kitchen counters, I guess."

She had been the one on the counter, but who was keeping track? "That's doable." Tongue in cheek, she promised, "If it will make you feel better, I'll stay out of kitchens with you entirely."

"Maybe that would work."

At the look of serious relief on his face, she didn't mention they were in one now. Or that their first kiss had happened in the entertainment room. Why burst his bubble?

"Well, then, shall we go apartment-hunting?"

He nodded. "Get your coat. I'll drive."

He definitely made a better driver than navigator, so she did not argue. Gathering the paper with her listings circled, her coat and her purse, she followed Grant out to the truck.

"Shoot." She shoved her purse and the paper toward Grant. "Here. Put these in the truck, will ya?"

"Where are you going?"

"I forgot to put the cats in the bathroom."

"Oh. Speaking of animals. Bud came out this morning."

She had forgotten entirely about the missing hamster. "Great. That's a relief."

"Yeah. He didn't seem damaged by his sojourn into my walls."

Zoe just hoped the same was true for Grant's wiring.

She found the cats and shut them in the bathroom, and then rejoined Grant in the truck. "Let's go."

He put the truck in gear. "Where to first?"

She named an apartment complex near the Dry Gulch. Grant could get his apology to Carlene out of the way. Looking in the backseat, she saw the beautiful crimson roses Grant had bought Carlene. It hardly seemed fair that Grant would bring her, Zoe, to a shattering climax and then give flowers to another woman.

Life was certainly twisted sometimes.

Grant must have noticed her eyeing the flowers.

"I bought them for her yesterday."

"I know."

"I should have given them to her when she insisted on going home, but I was too worried about Bud to think of it."

"Yeah."

"Damn it, Zoe. They *are* her flowers. I've got to give them to her."

"I never said you shouldn't."

"Right. Well. So long as you understand."

CHAPTER EIGHT

GRANT fought to concentrate on the road.

Zoe's presence and his uncertain feelings toward her distracted him. It really bugged him the way Zoe could go from falling apart in his arms one minute to disinterested sidekick the next. She *understood* his rules. Didn't complain about them. Didn't she know that women were supposed to feel used and abused when men did the things he had done with her in the kitchen without committing to at least a casual relationship?

Zoe acted like the entire incident was nothing more than a small blip in their friendship. She wasn't even mad that he was giving flowers to Carlene. He should be giving flowers to *Zoe*. Dozens of them. A man did things like that after experiences like the one they had shared.

It took what was left of his self-discipline not to demand an explanation for her behavior.

A little self-interest was mixed in as well. If he asked her what was making her respond with such insouciance to their passionate encounter, then she might expect him to explain what had happened. He wished he knew. The sight of Zoe hugging Tyler wearing nothing but a scanty piece of terry cloth had sent Grant right over the edge.

Rather than soothe him, her explanation had only made him angrier. More jealous. The feel of Zoe losing control in his arms had been so incredible he had forgotten everything but her.

Until Tyler and Jenny had come back.

Unfortunately, by then it had been too late. Grant was never going to forget the way it had felt to hold Zoe shivering in his arms. He gripped the steering wheel tightly. *Never.*

Zoe's prolonged silence finally registered. He shot her a sidelong glance. "You okay?"

She met his eyes briefly, the brown depths of her gaze hiding her thoughts from him. "I'm fine."

He nodded, refocusing his attention to the road. Right. "You want to check out the apartment complex while I stop by and get things straight with Carlene?"

"That's what I planned."

Great. So why did he feel like such a heel?

He dropped her off in front of an apartment complex across the street from the Dry Gulch. He didn't like the proximity to the bar, but vowed not to argue with her about it. Not unless she actually ended up wanting to rent the place.

Zoe stepped out of the rig. "I'll come over to the Dry Gulch when I'm done here."

"Okay. See you in a bit."

Grant walked into the dim interior of the country and western bar. His eyes took several seconds to adjust to the lack of light after the bright glare of sun off the snow outside. Tim McGraw was singing a ballad with his wife, Faith Hill, over the speaker system. The romantic words made him think of Zoe, and how *un*romantic he had been with her.

A man was not supposed to be romantic with his best friend—not if he wanted to keep the friendship intact. But what about the woman he spent a mind-blowing passionate encounter with? What about her? And what if they were one and the same? What was a man supposed to do then?

"Hey, Grant. Don't tell me those are for me?"

The sound of Carlene's soft Texas drawl interrupted his confused musings. She stood behind the bar, her smile covering more than the tight leather vest that passed as her top.

"I forgot to give them to you last night in all the hullabaloo over Bud."

She blushed. "That's so sweet. I felt like such an idiot, leaving and not helping you look for him."

"He came out on his own. Hamsters are small, but they're resilient." He set the flowers on the bar in front of her.

She leaned forward and sniffed them. "Mmmm. These smell wonderful. You're a real romantic, aren't you?"

Not if you asked Zoe. "I'm sorry about dinner."

"Me too. I really am." She leaned across the bar and touched his cheek, the movement strangely hesitant. "Why don't we try it again? This time at my place."

Oh, hell. He moved a step back, breaking the contact of her fingertips with his face. "I…uh…I can't leave Zoe's pets without supervision right now." The lie came out sounding as ridiculous as it was.

Carlene looked down at the roses and then back at him, her expression thoughtful. "Maybe we can work something out."

"Maybe." Even as he said the noncommittal word, the image of Zoe's face as she climaxed filled his mind.

Their friendship had been irrevocably altered that

morning, and pretending it hadn't wasn't going to change a thing. He did not want to be with any other woman, and it wasn't fair to Carlene, himself or Zoe to pretend otherwise. He opened his mouth to tell Carlene, but was interrupted by a man demanding another beer from the other end of the bar.

Carlene grimaced. "I'm sorry. I've got to go."

"No problem. Look, I—"

The customer banged loudly with his beer bottle on the bar and Carlene turned away without giving Grant an opportunity to finish his sentence. He'd have to call her later and let her know he wouldn't be dating anyone but Zoe from here on out.

He wasn't sure what Zoe would think of that. It hadn't been the most successful of endeavors when she'd been nineteen and he'd allowed himself to treat her like a woman instead of his best friend for a few mad weeks. The one time he'd let his passion get the better of him, she'd ended up looking like a wounded pup and running from him. He'd been very careful to keep his libidinous thoughts about her under lock and key since.

She hadn't looked shocked or dismayed in the kitchen, though. And why should she? She was a professional woman now, not an innocent teenager still in college. She'd come back to Sunshine Springs of her own volition. She had the career of her choice and she did not need to be protected from him any longer.

He didn't know why it had taken him so long to figure that out, but one thing was certain. His attempts to ignore the desire that was always one step away from bucking out of control like an unbroken horse had failed.

* * *

When he got outside, he scanned the street and parking lot of the Dry Gulch before noticing Zoe sitting in the truck cab.

He loped over to the navy blue rig and swung open the driver's door. "I thought you were going to meet me inside."

She tugged her knitted cap more firmly onto her head, tucking a stray strand of her pretty brown hair under it and behind her ear. "You were busy. I decided to wait here."

Why had she left the bar without saying anything? "I told you I had to apologize to Carlene."

Zoe pulled out the newspaper page with several red circles around ads, many of which had already been crossed out. "I think we should concentrate on older apartment complexes. They are more likely to allow pets. Let's go to the Courtyard. It's on the other side of town, near the county line."

Grant knew where Zoe was talking about, and just thinking about her living there was enough to sidetrack him from demanding a reason for her leaving the bar without saying anything. The apartments were in a small rundown complex near the one and only topless bar in the county. "No way."

She turned hostile brown eyes on him. "I've got to find a place to live, and most apartments won't take pets. The ones that will don't allow the number I have."

"You can't seriously consider living in the Courtyard."

"Right now, I'd consider just about anywhere."

"What about that place near the school?"

"No dogs."

He tossed out several more names and met with the same terse reply. *No.* He could understand her irritation. "I'm not taking you to the Courtyard."

"Where I live is my decision." Her bravado melted and she sighed. "It will just be for a little while anyway. I'll start looking for a house come spring."

He wondered what had changed her mind about buying a house. He didn't ask. Instead, he said, "There has to be someplace better, even if it is only temporary."

She frowned, her pixyish face set in mulish lines. "I don't want to waste the entire day looking at places that won't even consider me."

But that was exactly what they did. Over the next several hours they visited every apartment complex, room for rent and house for rent in the nearby county. No one wanted to rent to a woman who had a large dog, two cats, a hamster, a parrot and a goat.

Grant would not back down and take her to the Courtyard. They argued about it again when they ran out of alternatives.

"Zoe, living in a place like the Courtyard is not an option. I used my cellphone to call the Sheriff's office while you were talking to that couple about the duplex. They get calls to the Courtyard at least once a week."

She glared at him. "I'm not going to be causing any disturbances."

"Don't be stubborn." He knew he had hit rock-bottom with his arguments when he asked, "What would your parents think?"

Her silence spoke with more volume than any shouting match.

"Don't look like that. Just because they aren't coming home for Christmas doesn't mean they don't care about you." But he decided it was time he called her father and told the older man a few home truths—like that was exactly how Zoe saw their actions. He'd talked more intransigent men than Mr. Jensen into doing what he wanted, and he wanted Zoe's parents there for her at Christmas. "Your mom would flip if she knew you were even thinking about living there."

Zoe took the newspaper and folded it with exaggerated precision. She tucked it into the side pocket in the door of the truck, and then pulled her seatbelt across her small waist and buckled it. "Do you want to pick up dinner before you drop me off, or just take me home?"

She had always had a knack for changing the subject when she did not want to dwell on something. He sighed, and started the truck. "Dinner first. I'm starving."

He pulled out of the parking lot and headed toward Main Street and the few restaurants in Sunshine Springs.

She said, "Okay, but let's make it a drive-thru. I want to get home. I've got work to do, and the cats are probably sick to death of the bathroom."

He turned onto Main Street. "I have a better idea. Let's get pizza, pick up your cats and eat at my place. We can drive to the pageant together afterward, and let the cats roam free."

She looked out the window. "I was thinking about skipping the Nativity Play."

"I know you get nervous when your kids are on stage, but they're counting on you to be there."

Her almost child-size hands clenched in her lap. "You're right, but you don't have to go with me. I'm a grown-up. I don't need you along to hold my hand."

"Are you trying to get rid of me?" he asked jokingly.

"Yes."

He nearly ran one of the only two stoplights on Main. "Why?"

"I think you were right. We need to spend less time together. Tonight seems like the ideal place to start."

Fear washed over him like water from a mountain stream, leaving his heart cold in its wake. He'd decided to explore the possibilities of a relationship with her and she was pulling away. "I said the kitchen. We need to spend less time together in the kitchen."

Realizing how idiotic he sounded, he shut up. Damn. He'd known kissing Zoe would be a risk. He was losing her, and he wasn't even dating her yet. Had she already decided he wasn't worth compromising her lifestyle for?

His mother had made that decision when he was too young to understand but old enough to remember the pain. His ex-fiancée had followed the pattern his mom had set when she'd dumped him because he had opted to run the ranch rather than stay on the east coast. Even his stepmom, Lottie, was a prime example of the way women used marriage and love to tie men in knots and force them to change or be abandoned.

She'd given his dad an ultimatum: move to Portland and leave the ranch to be run by someone else, or lose her.

His dad had opted to keep his wife—unlike when Grant's mother had made a similar demand about returning to the east coast, where they had met on one of his frequent business trips. She hadn't liked life as a rancher's wife either. Living without the glittery nightlife she'd been used to had been too difficult an adjustment for her to make.

So she'd gone.

He pulled into a parking spot in front of the take-and-bake pizza place.

Zoe gave him a smile tinged with sadness. "That's not what you meant and we both know it."

It took him a minute to remember what they'd been talking about. When he did, he felt his insides tighten.

"What I know is that I'm not about to stop spending time with you." He gritted his teeth, but could not stop the words from coming out. "I need you, Zoe."

She frowned. "You have Carlene. You don't need me."

"I don't have Carlene."

"You're seeing her. I heard you in the bar."

"You heard Carlene ask me to reschedule our date?" Could that be what this cold shoulder was all about?

"Yes."

"You didn't eavesdrop long enough, then."

She huffed. "I was not eavesdropping."

He grinned. "Right. Look, *niña,* if you had stuck around a few seconds longer you would have heard me resort to dishonest measures to *avoid* another date with Carlene."

Her soft brown eyes mirrored wary hope. "I would?"

"Yes. I told her that I couldn't leave your pets alone."

Zoe laughed with disbelief. "Didn't she think it was odd that you were in town now if that were true? Not to mention the fact that you have a ranch full of hands, even if quite a few are spending time with their families right now?"

He shrugged. "I don't know."

The laughter died. "You gave her roses."

"I explained that. I bought them yesterday. Before."

She measured him with a look. "Before what?"

"Before we made out on the counter."

Her face turned crimson. "We didn't technically make anything."

He raised his brows and she bit her lip in embarrassment. "We didn't?"

"Well, maybe *I* did…"

"Yeah, I'd say you did. And if you'll let me, I'm going to real soon, too."

"Are you saying what happened to me on the Pattersons' kitchen counter changed the dynamics of our relationship or your relationship with Carlene?"

"Both." Didn't she feel the same way? If she wanted to forget what had happened, he didn't know how he was going to oblige her. Not when all he wanted to do was repeat the experience.

"I see."

"What do you see?"

"You no longer have a rule against kissing me."

"I'd say it went a whole lot deeper than that."

"Maybe." She opened her door and slid out of the truck. Sticking her head back inside, she asked, "Aren't you coming?"

It wasn't going to work this time. She was not changing the subject. "Yeah, I'm coming." But not the way he wanted to be right then.

He got out of the truck and walked around to where Zoe waited for him on the sidewalk in front of the take-out pizza place. "Well?"

She fiddled with something in her purse. "Well, what?"

He frowned, his chest tightening inexplicably. "Don't play games with me, Zoe. Did it change things for you too?"

She glanced behind him and smiled at someone. "Hello, Mrs. Givens."

Grant tensed at the sound of her former landlady's name. He had a few things he'd like to say to that old biddy, but right now he wanted an answer from Zoe more.

"Good afternoon, Zoe— Grant." Mrs. Givens stopped with every evidence of wanting to chat. "Finished with your Christmas shopping yet?"

He fixed his gaze on the older woman. "Zoe's been a

little busy looking for a place to live. She hasn't had time to do her shopping."

Zoe gasped and Mrs. Givens frowned. "I'm sorry to hear that. It was a very difficult decision to encourage Zoe to find a new place for her and her pets to live. However, I assumed that since I hadn't been called for a reference she had decided to move in with you at the ranch."

"Surely you've spoken to Mrs. Patterson?" Zoe said. "She must have told you that they've very generously allowed me to stay at their house while I look for a new place." Grant thought her voice sounded strained.

Mrs. Givens' eyes widened. "I haven't spoken to my dear friend since the night you left. I cannot imagine that she has allowed you to move your pets into her home."

Grant answered for Zoe. "She didn't. The animals are staying at my ranch."

"If I had known you would be willing to give up your pets, my dear, I would never have encouraged you to leave."

Like hell. The old biddy was lying through her teeth to make herself look better, but Grant wasn't fooled. He gave her the frozen look he usually reserved for boardrooms and drunken ranch hands. "Letting the animals stay at the ranch was *my* idea. You didn't leave Zoe with a lot of options when you *kicked her out.*"

Mrs. Givens drew herself up. "I could not condone rodents living in my house, and I was not merely referring to the animals staying at your house." She faced Zoe. "I read the advertisement looking for homes for your pets in the weekly."

He felt his body go tense. "You advertised for homes for your animals?" Damn it, she shouldn't have had to do that.

Zoe shrugged. "No one was going to rent to me with so many pets."

Mrs. Givens nodded her agreement. "Well, I've got a few more things to pick up before the shops close as well. I'll see you tonight at the pageant."

"Not if I can help it," Grant muttered as she walked away.

Zoe grinned at him. "Behave. I know you think you have to protect me from the world, but I'm perfectly capable of handling my former landlady."

He didn't return her smile. He didn't want to discuss Mrs. Givens. He didn't even want to talk about her giving up her pets. But he'd have something to say about that later. He wanted an answer to his earlier question, and he wasn't going anywhere until he got one. "Answer my question."

"Let's talk about this later, Grant." She gave him the smile that usually disarmed him. "I don't want to discuss what happened at the Pattersons' on a public sidewalk."

"I want to talk about it now."

Zoe's smile disappeared. "Well, I don't." She turned and walked into the take-and-bake pizza place. She marched up to the counter. "A double pepperoni calzone, please." She faced him. "What do you want?"

"An answer."

Her expression took on a hunted quality, and all five feet, two inches of her stiffened with her usual brand of stubborn resolve. "Later. Right now you need to order."

"I'll share your calzone. You can never eat a whole one." Before she could argue, he turned to the cashier. "Add an order of bread sticks and a large salad, please."

The kid behind the cash register gave Grant and Zoe a bored smile. "That'll be about fifteen minutes."

Grant said, "Fine." It shouldn't take more than a minute or two for her to answer his question. It wasn't that tough. Either their experience at the Pattersons' had changed their relationship for her, or it hadn't. He couldn't believe after the way she'd come apart in his arms that it hadn't, but he needed to hear her tell him so.

He grabbed her arm to pull her to one of the chairs that lined the small store's walls. "Did it, or didn't it?"

She crossed her arms over her breasts, drawing his attention to the curves under her coat. "It's not that simple."

"Yeah. It is. It's either *yes* or *no*. Which is it?"

She gave a pained smile to an elderly woman sitting next to her husband in the waiting area. She turned her gaze back to Grant. "I'm not sure we should change our relationship. Being friends has worked for a long time."

"You don't respond to my kiss like a friend, Zoe. You respond like a lover." The best lover he had ever had.

Her eyes skittered to the interested faces of the other patrons in the restaurant and she blushed. "Please, Grant, let's talk about this later."

He wanted her to admit that things had changed. "Just say yes or no."

"Yes." She shot up from her chair. "Yes. They've changed. But you aren't exactly a poster boy for commitment. I don't want to end up another notch on your bedpost."

He reached for her, but she yanked away. "I'll wait outside."

CHAPTER NINE

"A NOTCH on my bedpost?" They were the first words Grant had spoken about their argument since returning to the truck with their dinner.

The drive to the Double C had been a silent one, with her thinking about the ramifications of Grant wanting her to acknowledge a change in their relationship. Evidently he'd been mulling over her comment about bedposts.

Zoe felt her face heat. "You know what I mean."

"No. I guess I don't." He pulled her from where she stood spooning salad onto plates into the space between his jean-clad legs as he leaned against the counter. "We haven't even been to bed together. I can't notch anything."

"Don't be so literal." She didn't know why she was arguing this particular line of debate. She didn't want a commitment from Grant; she wanted to get rid of this desire that stopped her from wanting other men and seeing them as potential mates.

"I'm not *afraid* of commitment. I've been engaged once."

She looked him straight in the eye. "So you're saying you are looking at the possibility of marriage to me?"

His gaze shifted and his expression turned troubled. "I

don't know what the future holds, but I want to explore the possibilities between us."

Right. He wanted to go to bed with her. Somewhere between his horrified reaction to their encounter that morning and when they'd gone for dinner Grant's attitude toward having a physical relationship with her had changed. *He no longer had a rule against kissing her.* That did not mean he was looking at forever. *But she wasn't either*, she reminded herself.

She refused to acknowledge the emptiness inside her the thought provoked. Grant was offering her the thing she'd decided she wanted most—an opportunity to assuage the lust she felt for him. He wasn't offering love, but then neither was she. *She wasn't.*

"Okay."

"Okay, what?" He was looking at her with a distinct air of wariness.

"I'll go to bed with you."

He frowned. "Just like that?"

"Did you want me to play hard to get a while longer?"

His frown turned up a notch. "No. I'm just not sure what we're saying here."

"You're saying you want to go to bed with me, and I'm saying yes. It's pretty straightforward."

He didn't look convinced, but she didn't want to talk about it any longer. So she took the steps necessary to bring her body into frontal contact with his. She grabbed the back of his head and yanked. His mouth landed against hers with a gasp of surprised air. She took advantage and slipped her tongue inside to tease his. His response was everything she had hoped for.

He stopped trying to talk. She wasn't even sure he kept breathing. He planted his hands on her backside and lifted her until she hooked her legs around his waist, and then he kissed her back with a masculine passion that left her panting and her heart racing faster than the pace car at the Indianapolis 500.

She was enjoying their kiss so much that the annoying ring of the telephone did not immediately register. Grant peeling her from his body and pushing her gently away, however, did.

The phone shrilled once more, and with a look of apology Grant leaned past her to answer it. "I'm expecting a call from Mom and Dad," he explained as he lifted the receiver off the wall phone.

"Hello? Sure, just a minute." He handed the phone to her. "Your principal."

She cradled the phone against her ear. "Hello, John. What's up?"

"Hi, Zoe. I need to talk to you about something. Are you going to be at the Christmas Pageant tonight?"

"I'll be at the program, but can't we just talk about it now?" He had interrupted an incredible kiss, for heaven's sake. They might as well talk.

"I'd rather do this face-to-face, if you don't mind."

His serious demeanor was making her nervous. "What—am I fired or something?" She said it jokingly, but a small part of her was worried that it must be pretty serious for him to be unwilling to discuss it over the phone.

"Of course not." His immediate denial soothed her nerves. "We just have a small matter to work out. That's all."

"Is this about the bunny incident? I apologized to the other class, and I have been very careful to keep Pete in his cage since then."

"I hadn't heard about that. You'll have to enlighten me when we talk tonight."

Shoot—hadn't that police officer who'd pulled her over for a broken headlight told her never to volunteer information? That had been *after* he had asked her if she knew why she'd been pulled over and she had proceeded through a litany of ticketable offenses before he'd finally shut her up and told her to get a new headlight. Well, she was done offering information.

She'd wait to find out what was on John's mind tonight. "Fine. I'll see you there, then."

She hung up the phone and met Grant's gaze.

"What was that all about?" he asked.

She shrugged, her brows drawn together in thought. "I don't know. He wants to talk to me about something tonight at the program."

Grant pulled her back into the circle of his arms. "I take it he wasn't calling about the bunny incident?"

She smiled. "No."

All thought of bunnies and principals went out of her mind as Grant's lips fastened on hers again.

Zoe slid her gaze from the moonlight reflecting off the snow out the truck's window to Grant's profile. His handsome face took on a mysterious quality in the dim light. It was as if this man that she had known for most of her life had become a stranger. A sexy stranger.

She'd felt this way once before—the summer she'd been nineteen. She'd loved him then. Almost desperately. This time she just wanted his body—didn't she?

She'd given up on his heart after he'd hurt her so badly when she was nineteen, but the feelings roiling round inside her now felt like something more than lust. That scared her more than the conversation she'd had with her principal at the Christmas Pageant.

John had suggested she stop seeing so much of her best friend for a while, to let the gossip die down. Evidently rumors were circulating about her living with Grant...with the most intimate connotation of the words.

John had been more than a little worried about how the gossip would affect the reputation of the school, even after she had assured him she wasn't even living in *non*-connubial bliss with Grant. Part of her understood the school administration and board's attitude about the matter. Despite its influx of the rich and famous twice a year, Sunshine Springs was so small a town that building the second stoplight had been cause for a town dance and barbecue.

She'd seen a different way of life when she'd gone away to college, but she'd never been able to completely dismiss the morals she'd been raised to believe were right. Those morals did not include moving in with a man without the benefit of marriage. She knew the majority of the townspeople held similar ideas, particularly the parents of her five-year-old students.

John had been right about that. But she wasn't living with Grant and she refused to be punished for rumor rather than reality. She wasn't giving up her relationship with Grant for anyone, and she'd told her principal that very thing.

He hadn't been happy.

"You've been about as talkative as a sleeping bull since you and John talked after the pageant." Grant's words brought Zoe back from her reverie. "What's going on?"

She smiled. "I'm sorry. I didn't mean to ignore you. Really. I was thinking."

"I could tell. I want to know what you were thinking about. Are you having second thoughts about us?"

The vulnerability in his voice surprised her. "I'm not having second thoughts."

"Then what is it?"

"John had heard from some *reliable source* that I was living with you. He wanted me to know that the school administration, the school board and the parents of my students would all take a very dim view of such an arrangement."

Grant's head whipped around to face her. "Did he threaten your job?"

Zoe sighed. "Not in so many words. And I don't know how far he would have pushed it either, because I told him immediately that I'm staying at the Pattersons' and looking for a place of my own."

"What else?" He knew her so well. Someone else would have assumed that had been the end of the discussion, but Grant could read her too well.

"He's as concerned about the rumor as the reality. He wants me to cut back the time I spend with you to allay gossip," she said.

"Like hell." The words exploded in the truck cab like a Christmas firecracker. "What did you say?" There was that vulnerability again.

She put her hand on his thigh, reveling in the hard muscle and the sense of intimacy of the action. "I told him that I refused to have my private life dictated by the gossips in Sunshine Springs."

"Did he accept that?"

She started to draw little shapes with her finger on Grant's leg. "He wasn't thrilled, but he had no choice."

Grant's breathing quickened. He put his hand over Zoe's

to still it. "I'm going to drive us into a ditch if you keep that up." He squeezed her hand and went silent for about half a minute. "Maybe we should consider what John said. I don't like the idea of you being the brunt of gossip in town."

Frustration poured through Zoe. She hadn't stood up to her principal for Grant to go chicken-hearted on her. "Make up your darn mind. I'm tired of playing this tune. This morning you were so appalled by what happened in the kitchen that you wanted to curtail our friendship. Then you apparently chucked your whole rule about kissing me and your concerns about getting too close out the window."

She took a deep steadying breath. "You demanded that I acknowledge the change in our relationship, which I did. Now we're back to maybe we should not spend so much time together."

He pulled into the Pattersons' drive. He parked next to her truck, but didn't turn off the engine. "Let's talk about this tomorrow. It's been a long, emotional day for you, and you didn't get a lot of sleep last night."

She unbuckled her seatbelt and shoved her door open before jumping out. "Silly me—I thought the emotion was mutual today." She grabbed her purse off the seat and slammed the door.

She'd gotten the front door open before he caught up with her.

He spun her around to face him. He didn't say anything. He just slammed his mouth down on hers in an incinerating kiss. His lips were hard and demanding as they moved over hers, forcing a response even though she was still angry. She pressed her body against him in an instinctual move that felt pretty dang primitive.

He slipped his hands inside her coat, and it wasn't until

his fingers had closed over bare flesh under her sweater that she came to her senses. She struggled against him, dragging her mouth away from his. "Stop."

He kissed the side of her neck when she denied him her lips.

She pressed against his chest and shoved. "I mean it. Stop."

His breathing harsh, he did as she demanded.

She pulled from his arms. "I'm not going here again. I need some time to think. Apparently so do you."

He took a step back and dug his fingers through his dark hair. "Fine. You're right." He stepped toward his truck. "I'll call you tomorrow."

She nodded. She couldn't speak. Her throat was too tight. She watched him move toward the truck, her insides twisted in knots. He stopped when he reached the driver's side door.

"Zoe?"

"Yes?" The word came out as no more than a whisper, but he heard her.

"The emotion *was* mutual." Then he was gone.

Grant finished feeding the horses and headed back up to the house. He wanted to get in his truck and go to Zoe, but that wasn't an option. He'd called her this morning on the phone, figuring she'd had plenty of time to think about their relationship. She'd had all night. Evidently she hadn't spent it thinking about them. She'd had the gall to tell him that she had slept and slept well. He rubbed his tired eyes.

He hadn't. He'd spent the night tormented by images of Zoe on the countertop in the Pattersons' kitchen. Zoe coming apart in his arms. The hurt on her face when she'd thought he'd made a date with Carlene. The feel of Zoe's lips under his. He kept playing her reaction to his suggestion that they follow John's recommendation to protect her from gossip over in his mind. He couldn't get the look of wariness in her eyes when she'd told him they both needed time to think out of his mind.

Why had she been so upset last night? He'd only been trying to protect her. And why had she been so hesitant to admit the change in their relationship? He didn't like it that she needed time today to think about it either. Or that she'd refused to see him until she was ready.

She should be ready now.

To heck with it. She'd had all day. He was going over there and they were going to talk things out. Besides, he needed to tell her that Bud had been picked up by his new owner. Grant could have used the phone, but he'd rather tell her in person.

He wasn't going to say anything about the phone call he'd made not long after hanging up with her that morning, though. He'd called Mr. Jensen and read the older man the riot act. It was time the Jensens started treating Zoe like their valued daughter and not an afterthought. The older man was too stubborn to promise to change his plans, but Grant could tell he'd been shaken by the things Grant had said.

If the two didn't show up for Christmas he would be surprised, but he wasn't warning Zoe about the possibility on the off chance he was wrong. She would only be hurt more then.

He slammed into the house, leaving the back door open. He went to grab his truck keys from the hook by the door, but at the sound of tires crunching over the snow on his drive his hand froze midway. She'd come to her senses. He looked out the back window. Carlene's stylish compact came into view. It halted a few feet from his back door.

Oh, hell. He'd forgotten to call her and set things

straight. After giving vent to his frustration with a few well-chosen words, he went outside to face the music.

"Hello, Carlene."

She turned on her high-heeled boot and gave him a strangely tentative smile. "Hi. I got off work early tonight, and instead of going home I thought I'd bring dinner. To make up for the other night, you know?"

"Look, there's something I need to tell you."

She shivered. "Can you tell me inside? It's freezing out here."

"Sure."

She started taking off her coat when they got inside, and innate courtesy had him reaching out to help her. The words he wanted to say stalled in his throat as he became aware of what Carlene was wearing under the coat.

Her boots stopped at her ankles and fishnet covered the rest of her bare legs. Her dress looked more like a shiny Spandex slip. The way she kept tugging on the hem was probably meant to draw his attention to her skimpily clad thighs. The top of the dress was skin-tight and off the shoulder. If she was wearing a bra, it had to be the size of a Band-Aid. Nothing else would fit under the snug fabric.

Her lips curved in a smile that looked a little ragged around the edges. What was going on?

"Like it?" she asked.

What the hell was he supposed to say to that? All he could think of was that if Zoe walked in now, he was a dead man. "Isn't that a little cold for this time of year?"

She sidled up to him and trailed her fingers down his shirtfront. "It's my working gear, but I'm counting on you to keep me warm."

He stepped back hastily, before she could get any more ideas. The thought had him jumpier than a colt in his first batch of snow. "I'll turn up the heat."

Her laughter trilled over his stressed nerves, sounding more forced than seductive. "I'm counting on it." She undid the top button on his flannel shirt with trembling fingers.

Grant stumbled backwards and escaped into the hall. Rejecting a woman's advances never got any easier. It went right against the strictures his dad had drilled into him about courtesy toward women since Grant had been old enough to notice the difference between the sexes.

He stood staring at the thermostat stupidly, forgetting what he had come into the hall to do—besides get away from Carlene. Taking several deep breaths, he reminded himself that he was a man and in control of the situation.

Yeah. Right.

When it came to women, men were rarely in control.

He walked back into the kitchen and stopped short at the darkness. Carlene had extinguished the lights and lit two candles on the counter. "What the…? I can't do dinner. I'm sorry. I was just about to leave when you showed up."

Her smile faltered and then came back, turned up a notch. "Maybe you could put off your errand for a little while?"

"We need to talk." He started backing up toward the light switch.

Her eyes flared with what looked like hurt at his rejection.

His shoulder hit the wall and he desperately searched for the light switch. His grateful fingers closed over it and he pushed upward. The kitchen flooded with light.

Carlene jumped, her eyes blinking at the bright fluorescent light. Under the bright light of the kitchen she looked tired…and sad.

He hated what he had to say next. "I should never have asked you out in the first place."

"Are you in a relationship?"

"Not exactly." Not until Zoe said he was. "But I want to be."

"Oh." Her expression was pained. "I'm sorry I misread your signals. The roses…" She sighed. "You know?"

"It's not your fault."

She nodded, obviously agreeing with him, and turned to go. That was when the lights went out, quickly followed by the high-pitched whine of the fire alarm.

"Hell."

"What is that?" Carlene shouted.

"My fire alarm."

"There's a fire?"

"No," he shouted over the alarm. Remembering how the light had gone off on its own, he yelled, "There must be a short in the wires or something."

The hiss of escaping water put the cap on Grant's endurance. "Get out of here!" he yelled.

Carlene was already headed for the door. It didn't save her. The automatic sprinkler system went off and both Carlene and Grant were drenched in seconds. Grant headed for the phone on the counter. If he didn't call the fire station immediately, he'd have a whole lot more to worry about than a wet floor.

It took two tries to get the receiver, slippery with water, to stay in his hands before he could dial the number. Thankfully, he got through immediately, and explained that his place was not on fire.

Leaving Carlene in the kitchen, where it was warmer, if not drier than outside, since she was soaked to the bone,

Grant sloshed outside to find the emergency shut-off switch. After only six tries, he got it to turn off. He stepped back into the house, relieved that the high-pitched wailing had finally stopped.

The blessed silence was interrupted by the sound of another rig coming down his drive.

This time Grant's insides churned with dread rather than anticipation. It would be Zoe. He had no doubt. When her truck came into view he just stood there, like a man ready to face his executioner. Only he wasn't ready.

Zoe stopped the truck three feet from Carlene's car and got out. She glanced briefly at the car, and then at him. Her eyes widened when they took in his waterlogged state. "What happened?"

"Fire alarm."

Carlene chose that moment to make her appearance in the open doorway. Mascara ran down her face like an athlete's black line gone amok. Her hair was plastered like wet string against her skull, and she was glaring at him as if he had set off the alarm on purpose.

After the mess he'd made of things, he couldn't blame her.

A choked exclamation from Zoe had his attention careening away from the woman glaring at him. He turned to face Zoe.

"I didn't realize that you had company." Her even tone belied the stricken expression in her eyes. "I came by to tell you Tyler will be out to pick up the parrot sometime tomorrow. At least something good came from yesterday."

Was she trying to say that the change in their relationship *wasn't* good? He wouldn't accept that. "It's not what it looks like. I didn't know she was coming."

Zoe didn't say anything. She turned to leave and he

chased after her, grabbing her arm. "I mean it, Zoe. I was planning on coming to see you when she showed up."

He turned back to Carlene and demanded, "Tell her."

Carlene swiped at her wet hair. "So she's the one, huh?"

Zoe tried to yank her arm away. "No."

He blew out a frustrated breath and wouldn't let go. "Yes."

Carlene's gaze met Zoe's. "He's telling the truth. I came out tonight on a whim. I felt bad about the way I left last time, and I didn't realize the two of you had become an item. If it will make you feel any better, he made it clear from the start he wasn't interested. I didn't mean to hurt anyone. I'm sorry."

Some of the tension drained from Zoe, but she still tugged against his restraining hold. He let go.

She turned and started walking toward her truck again. His insides froze. "Zoe?"

It came out like a plea and he didn't care.

"Call me when you aren't otherwise engaged," she tossed back over her shoulder when she reached the driver's door. Then she left.

Carlene sighed. "I didn't mean to cause problems between you two. If I'd known it was like that I wouldn't have come. I probably shouldn't have come anyway."

"We'll work it out." He hoped. "I'm sorry if I misled you with my actions."

She shrugged. "These things happen. But if I were you, I wouldn't make a habit of giving flowers, especially roses, to one woman when you want another one."

"I won't." But he had no idea if the one he wanted to give flowers to would accept them from him.

CHAPTER TEN

THE smell of bleach burned Zoe's nostrils as she finished scrubbing the bathtub and then rinsed it.

She peeled off the bright yellow rubber glove from her right hand and swiped at her forehead. "Whew."

The cats were hiding somewhere. They knew better than to get in her way when she was in a cleaning frenzy.

She'd already tried venting, but it hadn't helped. Forty-five minutes of girl-chat with Jenny had only served to fan the outrage Zoe had felt, driving up to Grant's home and finding him and Carlene in what could only be termed a compromising circumstance. Jenny had reminded her that Grant had caught Zoe and Tyler in a similar situation and it had been innocent.

It hadn't helped. It wasn't the same. There was too real a risk that Grant had wanted Carlene there, even if he hadn't invited her. After all, he'd invited her once before.

The pain in her chest was way too familiar. She'd felt exactly like this four years ago, when Grant had dropped her off at home in order to take that New York model on a romantic evening flight in his plane. She'd cried for two solid hours that night. She refused to cry this time.

The stinging in her eyes had everything to do with the bleach she was using to clean and nothing to do with overactive tear ducts. She took a deep breath and held it, trying to assuage the very physical ache in her chest. It shouldn't hurt this much. She wasn't in love with Grant like she had been when she was nineteen.

The air hissed from between her lips as she let it out and drew another quick breath. *She wasn't.* Only a total idiot would let herself love a man who had rejected her so completely once already and had given red roses to another woman. Sure, he'd tried to justify it, but the details hadn't done a thing to explain why he'd asked Carlene out in the first place.

Grant had said their relationship had changed for him, but he'd also grabbed at the first opportunity to back off. He'd been all too willing to follow her principal's advice and spend less time together. Not a week ago he'd had a rule against kissing her. Why?

And why did thinking about him and Carlene hurt so much? Zoe should be angry, not hurt. After all, it was supposed to be physical for her—a way to get over the desire for Grant that had plagued her since she was sixteen.

Her emotions were not supposed to be involved.

She yanked her glove back on and surveyed the bathroom, looking for something else to clean. The small room sparkled more than it ever had when she'd cleaned it for her mom, when her family had lived in this house.

And she still felt the ache in her heart.

She had already vacuumed every inch of the Pattersons' home. Even the rooms she had left closed up. She had scrubbed down the counters in the kitchen, the floors, the windows and the mirrors. She pushed herself to do one more thing, to clean the last little nook, hoping that in doing so she would fall exhausted into bed tonight.

Then perhaps she would not lie awake for hours, tormenting herself with thoughts of Grant and Carlene.

Sighing, she peeled off her gloves and sat on the toilet seat. *Right.* She could work sixteen hours shoveling horse manure and she'd still go to bed and dream about Grant, with the dreams becoming nightmares mixed with memories from four years ago now Carlene had entered them.

The insistent chime of the doorbell penetrated her acidic thoughts. She considered not answering. Maybe whoever it was would go away. She knew it wasn't Tyler this time, because he'd been with Jenny when Zoe called. Which left Grant.

She'd told him to call her, not come by. She wasn't up to seeing him.

She tucked her feet up on the toilet seat and locked her arms around her knees, staring at the opening to the hall and willing him to leave. Loud pounding was interspersed with repeated peals from the doorbell. She tried covering her ears, but the sounds penetrated. She glared at the bucket of cleaning supplies, but they weren't going to help her—unless she planned to get rid of him with a squirt from the ammonia bottle.

She pushed herself up and went to answer the door.

Opening it a crack, she peered out.

She'd been right. It was Grant. "Open the door, Zoe. It's damn cold out here."

"I don't want to talk to you."

"That's too bad, because I'm not leaving." His tone had the implacability of a rock wall. "You might as well open up and let me in."

The thought of sending him away hurt more than the prospect of talking to him, so she obeyed, and then stood in shocked amazement at the sight before her. She could barely see Grant for all the flowers he held in his arms. He had at least three dozen roses in different shades, a bunch of colorful blooms made into a bouquet cradled in one arm and a potted mini-rosebush clutched in his free hand.

"Do you think I could come in?"

She stepped back and let him inside.

"Where do you want these?"

"Are they for me?" She wasn't taking anything for granted.

"Who else would they be for?" When she just stared at him, his mouth set in a firm line. "Don't answer that. Just tell me where to put them."

She led him into the kitchen. "I'll look for some containers."

She found a box of wide-mouth quart-size mason jars with Mrs. Pattersons' canning supplies. Zoe used them for the roses and the colorful bouquet. Grant went back outside and returned with several more bouquets and potted flowers. She put the mini-rosebush and other live plants on the counter next to the sink. When she was done, and Grant had made one more trip out to his truck, Mrs. Patterson's kitchen resembled a florist shop.

"What's this all about, Grant?"

His blue eyes speared her with their intensity. "It's about giving the right signals. I didn't want there to be any more confusion."

"You mean it's not an apology for me catching you entertaining Carlene dressed like a male fantasy come true?"

He frowned, running his tanned fingers through the

thick blackness of his hair. "No. I didn't invite her over. I know you believe me about that."

His eyes dared her to disagree with him. She didn't. The fact she believed he hadn't invited Carlene over didn't make the memory of the other woman standing in his doorway wearing fishnet stockings any less painful.

His gaze speared her. "The only fantasy come true for me is you…dressed any way at all…but undressed would be even better."

Her heart jogged and her betrayer of a body jolted at his words. "Then why did you bring the flowers?"

"Like I said, I wanted to give the right signals."

"What do you mean by signals?"

"A man shouldn't give flowers to one woman when he wants another one. It sends mixed signals."

Zoe looked around the kitchen at the plethora of flowers surrounding her. Warmth spread throughout her insides, but she remained wary. "And does the amount of flowers indicate in any way how much you want a woman?"

His eyes glittered midnight-blue in the fluorescent light and he started toward her. "I don't know, but I bought out the floral department at the grocery store to be on the safe side. I would have bought out the florist too, but they were closed."

"So, what happened tonight?" She backed up a step when he would have touched her. "Why did Carlene come over if you didn't invite her?"

"Mixed signals."

The roses. "I see. I guess you won't be giving other women flowers for a while, huh?" At least as long as their affair lasted.

He took another step closer, crowding her. "Right."

"What set off your sprinkler system?" She avoided

meeting his eyes and focused on the yellow roses in the mason jar on the counter opposite.

"I don't know."

But they could both guess. Bud. "I'm sorry. It's my fault, isn't it?"

He reached out and pressed his big hand to the side of her face, gently turning her head until their gazes met. His expression was as serious as a heartbeat. "It doesn't matter."

Her breathing reflex short-circuited and she had to concentrate on sucking air into her lungs. "Of course it matters. Bud probably ate your wiring, and I'm the one who let him out of his cage."

His thumb brushed down her chin and settled lightly against the pulse in her neck. "I don't care."

"But—"

"The only thing I care about is your promise to make love to me." He leaned down until their breath mingled.

She fought hard to concentrate on what they were saying. "I thought you wanted to back off for a while."

"I wanted to protect you. It's an instinct I have a hard time ignoring. But if it means losing you I'll ignore it—and anything else that could send you away from me."

"Even gorgeous models from New York?" She couldn't keep the residual pain from her voice. Her refresher course in that emotion was too recent.

His eyes narrowed while his mouth stopped a centimeter from her own. "What are you talking about?"

She tipped her head back, straining her neck to gain some distance. "It just seems to me that on the two occasions when you and I might have taken our friendship into the realm of the physical, you went for another woman instead."

"What do you mean by *might have*? Are you saying you

don't want to make love to me? If you are, then think again. Things have gone too far for us to turn back to our old platonic relationship."

"That's what I thought when I was nineteen, but I was wrong then and maybe you're wrong now." She wanted to make love with Grant, but some irresistible compulsion was prompting her to rehash old memories and hurts.

"Four years ago neither one of us was ready for this."

"Well, you certainly weren't. It would have meant giving up the model."

Suddenly she found herself sitting on the counter, a plethora of flowers and plants surrounding her, the smell of damp soil and the fragrance of flowers in bloom teasing her senses while Grant made a place for himself between her spread legs. "I didn't *have* the model."

"Come on, Grant. You took her for a midnight ride in your plane. What else were you going to do when you brought her back to the ranch?"

"Take her home."

She let her expression speak her disbelief for her.

"Zoe, I took Madeleine up in the plane so I wouldn't take you to an empty line shack and finish what we'd started in the barn. I didn't want to have sex with her."

For four years Zoe had taunted herself with the image of Grant and the willowy blonde in a clinch, and now he was telling her he had not even slept with the woman.

"Then why did you reject me?"

Confusion clouded his eyes. "Reject you? I never rejected you. You're the one who ran from the barn wearing an expression that accused me of damn near attacking you."

"I never did!"

He just stared at her.

"Okay. So, I ran. I'd never experienced anything like that before. It scared me, and I wasn't ready to make love for the first time."

"That's what I said earlier."

"But I got ready."

His hands settled on her thighs. "What do you mean?"

"I wanted to make love with you that night you took Madeleine up in your plane, after dropping me off at home like a pesky younger sister."

"Well, you couldn't have wanted it very damn bad. You left for college two days later—a full month before you had to be back for classes. And you didn't come home for a long visit again until you moved back a year ago."

Old anger and hurt welled up inside. "What did you expect me to do? Stick around and watch you have an affair with the bimbo model after treating me like your girl-friend for several weeks?" She shoved against his chest. "Let me down."

He didn't move an inch. "No way. We're talking this out."

"What's the point? It happened years ago. It's over and done with."

"If it were over for you, you wouldn't have brought it up."

He was right, darn it. "Okay. Tell me again why you took Madeleine up in your plane if you didn't want her, and while you're at it try explaining why you had a rule against kissing me and why you asked Carlene out."

He wanted a conversation? He could do the talking as far as she was concerned.

He opened his mouth and then closed it, an arrested expression coming over his face. "I did it all for the same reason. To protect you and our friendship."

"Oh, right."

His grip on her thighs tightened, reminding her that talking wasn't the only thing on Grant's mind. "You weren't ready to make love when you were nineteen. You even admitted it. I knew if I didn't do something, I'd end up seducing you."

"And seducing me would have been bad?"

"Yes. You were nineteen. A teenager. Totally innocent. And if that weren't enough you had two years left of college and a career choice that could have taken you anywhere in the country after you graduated."

Well, she was twenty-three now, but she was still pretty innocent. She wasn't in college any longer, but her career could still take her away…if she wanted it to. She didn't want to leave Sunshine Springs, but apparently Grant didn't know that. "I came back to Sunshine Springs and you still had that stupid rule against kissing me."

He smiled wryly. "I was still stuck in that mode of protecting you from my evil desires. It's a tough instinct to fight once embedded in the male psyche, and I've been protecting your feelings one way or another for the better part of my life."

"And Carlene?"

"I'd done a pretty good job of forgetting how much I wanted you, but all of a sudden everything about you turned me on—and I knew if I didn't do something I was going to seduce you."

Everything about her turned him on? Her fingers trembled as she laid them over his hand on her thigh. "And seducing me would still be a bad thing?"

"I thought so—at first. But then I realized two things."

"What?"

"One, you aren't nineteen anymore."

"Four years of living will do that."

He leaned his forehead against hers. "Yeah."

"And the second thing?"

"I can't resist you."

"But you resisted Madeleine and Carlene?"

"Absolutely, and without any problem."

A sudden thought stopped her from closing the distance between their mouths. "What about Bud and the parrot?"

His laugh sounded something like a strangled groan. "I didn't get a chance to tell you, but Tyler has already come by for the bird and your student's dad picked up Bud this afternoon."

"That's good."

He nodded, but said nothing, his intensity surrounding her like a physical presence. She opened her mouth to say something else—she wasn't sure what—but his lips cut off anything she might have said. Passion exploded inside her like a launching space shuttle, fire and sound roaring through her with amazing force.

The second his tongue touched her lips she opened for him. He groaned his approval and pulled her body into his, holding her still for one slanting kiss after another as the urgency behind each one increased with every subtle shift of his lips.

He placed hot open-mouthed kisses against her chin and throat. "You smell like bleach."

She laughed, the sound coming out strangled. "I've been cleaning."

He tunneled his fingers in her hair and kissed her ear, tickling her with his tongue. It was a good thing she was sitting on the counter because her leg muscles had turned to water.

He tugged her hair out of the ponytail holder she'd used to keep it out of her face while she was tidying up. "I didn't know household cleaning products could be so erotic."

"Me neither."

He didn't reply. His mouth was too busy tantalizing her collarbone. She didn't mind. In fact, she threw her head back to give him better access. "I like that."

"You don't taste like bleach. You taste so damn sweet. Just like I fantasized."

"You fantasized about me?"

He licked the column of her neck and she shivered. "Yeah."

Remembering what he had said when he'd first got there, she asked, "Was I naked in these fantasies?"

"Yes. I never forgot the sight of you without your top that one time we went crazy together in the barn."

That was nice. She melted back into his embrace, eager for another of his searing kisses.

Talking about it was making Grant desperate to feel her naked flesh. Flowers weren't the only things he'd bought at the grocery store. He leaned forward and scooped her up in his arms.

She gasped. "What are you doing?"

"Taking you to bed." He leaned down to kiss her again. She averted her face, so he concentrated on her neck while making his way to her bedroom. He walked in and dropped her on the bed. He started stripping out of his clothes.

She began to unbutton her blouse, and he stopped moving just to watch her.

She stilled. "You're watching me."

"I want to see you. All of you." With a body as beautiful as hers, she should expect it—or had she always made love in the dark?

Her cheeks turned a very pretty shade of pink. "I want to see you too, but there's something I need to tell you."

"What?"

"You know how tonight seems so much like four years ago?"

Except for the fact that tonight he was going to have Zoe, and four years ago he had only dreamed about it. "Yes."

"Well, it's a lot more like it than you might expect."

"What do you mean?" If she didn't get to the point soon, he wasn't sure he'd have the patience to let her.

"I was prepared to give you my virginity that night, Grant."

He realized that was why she had been so hurt. "I wish I had known, *querida*. I would have handled things differently."

"That's the point. I need you to know now."

His breath stilled in his chest. "Are you saying you are still a virgin? None of the men you dated in college and since…?"

"No."

His knees threatened to buckle. She'd never had another man. She belonged to him. Completely.

"I…" He didn't know what to say. Emotion welled up, clogging his throat.

She finished unbuttoning her shirt. "Promise me something?"

"Anything." He was so overwhelmed with his desire to touch her that nothing else registered.

She peeled out of her shirt and his fingers literally trembled with the need to touch the sweet flesh she'd exposed. She stopped with her hands on the front clasp of her bra. "Promise that you won't regret this."

Regret it? He wanted her more than anyone or anything

he had ever desired in his life. "The only thing I regret is how long you're taking to get out of your clothes."

He loved the way her breath hitched at his words. "No more talk about spending time apart?"

He frowned. How could she even suggest such a thing? They were about to make love. Her for the first time. And he liked that more than he should. "You know I only said that because I was worried about your reputation. I wanted to protect you."

She smiled. "We'll have to discuss that tendency of yours sometime, but not right now." She unclasped her bra.

He was out of his jeans in seconds.

He stopped his rush across the room when her wide brown eyes looked at his erection with a certain amount of trepidation. "It's going to be okay, baby. I'll be gentle."

She swallowed, and then shifted her gaze to his eyes. "I know. I trust you." She opened her arms to him.

He dived across the space that separated them, wanting to touch her, to taste the nipples that peaked at him like raspberries on top of two scoops of luscious, sweet, French vanilla ice cream.

She gasped when he landed on her with a thud. He smiled, feeling like a predator blessed with the sweetest prey ever sighted. "Sorry. Did I hurt you?"

"No." She sounded breathless, but not nervous, and for that he was very, very grateful.

He shifted his weight to his forearms and started kissing her again. She hadn't made it out of her jeans, and they rubbed against the bare skin of his thighs and his hardened male flesh, making him burn. He skimmed his hand down her shoulder, then over her chest, until he cupped the fullness of her breast against his palm. Its soft resiliency intoxicated him.

She groaned, and bucked against him with her hips.

He lifted his mouth from hers and looked down, drinking in the sight of his hand against her breast. "Zoe, *mi precioso,* you are so damn beautiful."

Zoe stilled beneath him and he looked up to her face. Crystalline tears trembled on her lashes.

He sucked in his breath. "You okay?" She didn't move. "What's the matter? What did I say?"

Maybe he was rushing things. She hadn't seemed nervous, but maybe she was.

"You think I'm beautiful?" Her smile did as much to warm him as her naked body beneath him. He bent his head and kissed each eyelid, brushing her tears with his lips.

"I have always thought you were beautiful."

"You never said so." Her voice trembled with emotion that Grant did not understand.

"That's not true. I've always told you I thought you were the prettiest girl in Sunshine Springs."

She sniffed. "But that was because you were my friend."

"It was because it was true. But it wasn't enough, was it?" He brushed his index finger over her pebbled nipple. "You're beautiful. Pretty doesn't cut it." He wanted to taste her. Moving down until he could take the sweet little bud in his mouth, he reveled in her silky skin. "You are so soft."

She groaned and bowed under him, pressing her breast against his lips. "Grant, I want you to touch me everywhere."

He was more than willing to oblige. He started by nibbling on the tender, creamy flesh surrounding the wet morsel he'd been suckling.

She nearly came off the bed. "Don't stop. Oh, please, don't stop."

He caressed her shoulders, her rib cage, and reached

under her to squeeze her bottom. Her hands twisted in his hair, pulling his head tight against her breast, silently begging for more of the same.

"Oh, Grant, oh, Grant, oh, Grant."

Exultation filled him at the need he heard in her voice. He lifted his mouth and she protested. He smiled at her. "Don't worry. I'm not done yet, but you still have too many clothes on."

He levered himself off of her and immediately set about unbuttoning her jeans. He unzipped them and then put his hands on her waistband, ready to tug them off. She lifted her hips for him. She wiggled until he got the denim past her derriere. He stopped. He could not help it. The scrap of turquoise silk covering her most intimate place paralyzed him.

She looked at him with a question in her eyes.

He licked lips suddenly gone dry. "Do you realize what a privilege this is? How honored I feel that you chose me to be your first lover, *querida*?"

"That's nice—but could you get on with it?" She wasn't smiling, because he knew she wasn't trying to tease him. She meant it, and that did things to him. Her eyes were filled with heated desire. "I feel like I'm going to die waiting for you," she moaned.

He smiled and felt things inside him shift. Where he had been mindless with his desire to couple with her, he now had an overwhelming need to cherish her first. To show her how much he appreciated the gift of being able to touch her and be with her.

Of being her first lover.

CHAPTER ELEVEN

"GRANT?"

He slid her pants an inch down her thighs. "Yes?"

"Um, are you going to take off my jeans, or what?"

He loved the sound of impatience in her voice, loved knowing he was doing this to her. "Oh, I'm going to take off your jeans, all right. Relax, Zoe. I want to cherish you."

She put her hands over his and pushed on her jeans. "Cherish me naked, okay?"

He laughed, the sound strangling in his throat. "I guess I can do that."

Moving back to the edge of the bed by her feet, he pulled her pants off and stood back to appreciate the sight of her in nothing but the little scrap of fabric covering her most feminine place. She was so beautiful and, at least for right now, she was his. Totally and completely.

He leaned forward and kissed her stomach, letting his tongue explore the indentation of her belly button, reveling in the way she writhed below him. She was so responsive and still a virgin. Somehow he knew, even if she didn't, that she had been waiting for him.

Kissing a trail over her smooth skin, he stopped when he reached the top of her panties. Taking them in his teeth and hooking his fingers on the waistband at either side, he pulled them off.

Slowly. Very, very slowly.

She groaned and squirmed, trying to get her legs free, but he kept her captive with the panties as he continued down the naked flesh of her legs centimeter by centimeter.

She shouted his name and he felt a sense of primitive male power surge through him. She wanted him. Damn, it felt good. He finally brought the scrap of silk over her ankles and then her feet. Standing up, he dropped them on the floor.

The sight of her naked body on the rumpled bedding once again paralyzed him. He had sublimated the feelings rushing through him for so long, it was almost impossible to believe he was here, in Zoe's old bedroom, with Zoe lying on the bed wearing nothing but a dusky red blush.

He'd had other women, but he could never remember feeling like this. This was more than physical. Hell, it was more than mere emotion. There was something spiritual about making love to this woman.

He met her eyes and smiled. "You're blushing."

Her lips twisted in a shy frown. "You're staring at me."

"I can't help it. You're so perfect." Didn't she realize that?

"I'm not perfect."

He gave her a considering look. "Yes, you are. Let me show you." He picked up her foot and started giving nibbling kisses to each tiny digit. "Your feet are so sexy that just the sight of this little toe—" he wiggled her pinky toe "—gets me so hot my jeans get uncomfortable."

She stared at him, her mouth opened slightly, her brown eyes dark with emotion.

He gave her instep an open-mouth kiss, letting his

tongue tickle it before pulling back. "You've got a really erotic arch, *niña*. You could do feet commercials."

"Feet commercials?" Her voice broke in the middle of the word *commercials*.

"Uh-huh." His lips moved their way up her calves to the inside of her knee. Her breathing became ragged. So did his. He knew where he was going and, by the tensing of her thighs, he figured she did too.

"Grant?"

"Sweetheart, you've got legs that could stop traffic. I have never appreciated your particular style of dress as much as I do at this moment. If you wore short skirts, I wouldn't get any work done. I'd spend all my time staring at your sexy knees." He punctuated each word with a kiss on one of her legs.

"Sexy knees? I didn't know anyone had sexy knees."

He shrugged. "Like I said, you're perfect."

Then he zeroed in on his target, gently parting her swollen flesh with his tongue and licking the slick little bud at the apex of her femininity. Zoe's hips strained up off the bed and she screamed. He flicked her with his tongue while inserting a finger slowly into her hot, moist, very tight passage. He wanted this to be perfect for her.

He wanted her to remember this night as the most wonderful experience of her life.

"Grant!" His name sounded like both a demand and a plea.

He gave in to both and pulled her swollen button of love into his mouth, suckling it like he had her nipple earlier. Her scream reverberated through his body like an electric charge.

"Please, please, *please*…"

Did she even know what she was begging for? What he planned to give her? She bucked against him and he continued kissing her intimately, until he could taste her sweet honey flow and she shuddered with release against his mouth. She cried out again, a high-pitched scream that went on for several seconds. He didn't stop his ministrations and she thrashed against the bed, trying to dislodge him and press herself more firmly against him all at the same time.

She came again, this time sobbing his name, and then just sobbing. The swollen tissues of her sex contracted around his finger and he almost came, thinking what that was going to feel like when he was inside her.

He kept on until she begged him to stop, and her body went completely limp around him, convulsing sporadically when his tongue hit a particular spot of soft feminine flesh. He gentled her with the soothing touch of his fingers and soft kisses pressed against the sensitized flesh at the juncture of her thighs.

He stood up and donned a condom. She watched him put on the protection, her eyes slumberous with spent passion.

He smiled, but his heart felt tight. This act was so important. It had never been this way with another woman, but he felt as if taking Zoe would be permanent. It was more than being her first lover. It was knowing that she belonged to him on a fundamental level he couldn't begin to explain. She always had, but he'd been too stubborn to admit it.

A desire that did not die after four years of suppression was not born of lust. He shied away from identifying what had given it birth. It was enough to know that this was something special.

Zoe could not believe that her body was once again responding to the sight of Grant's arousal. The way he'd brought her to multiple orgasms with his mouth had totally exhausted her—or so she'd thought. Now she felt the stirrings of renewed need, as well as a deep longing to satisfy her lover every bit as thoroughly as he had satisfied her.

She didn't doubt she could do it, even if she'd never had a lover before. She'd read books—and not just erotic romance either. She'd read sex manuals when she'd been trying to find a way to want a man besides her best friend. But now that problem was solved. It was Grant standing so sexily above her, so obviously ready to join his body with her own.

How could she help but satisfy him? She longed to give him every bit of pleasure her body was capable of providing.

She smiled in welcome as Grant lowered himself over her, pressing the head of his erection against the sensitized flesh of her femininity. Her legs widened of their own accord to make a place for him.

"I want you."

"I'm glad, *querida*." His voice sounded strained.

She arched her hips against him and the head of his shaft slipped inside. He groaned and pressed into her, but she was tight and he was big. Bigger than she'd expected. She bit her lip and did a little shimmy with her hips, which allowed him another inch of access.

She tried to relax, but she felt so stretched. Yet the sensation of his invading manhood felt so right that she vacillated between wanting all of him and fearing that she couldn't take it. She could only say a prayer of thanks that she'd been riding horses since she was three. There was no fleshly barrier that had to be torn for him to gain entrance, no source of pain to mitigate the pleasure of their joining.

He rocked against her, pressing inexorably closer, and her swollen tissues gave all at once, allowing him to seat to the hilt. She moaned. The sensation of his hard shaft inside of her and the press of his pelvic bone against her splintered her thoughts and tormented her senses.

"Oh, Grant."

"I know, Zoe. I know."

She didn't know if she could stand it if he moved, but she wanted it. Oh, man, she wanted it. *"Grant."*

He seemed to read her mind, because he pulled back and rocked forward in a withdraw-and-plunge move that rasped every nerve-ending in her feminine core. Pushing her legs together and settling his outside, he forced his hardness against her clitoris with every thrust. She felt the excitement building again, even more shattering than when his mouth had been on her.

She tried to move under him, and succeeded in small pelvic thrusts that seemed to drive him wild. Grant's movements became more forceful, until he was driving into her like a jackhammer. Her body tightened like a bow, pushing against his muscular length, forcing him to fight her for the embrace. Which he did, with amazing success, pushing her closer and closer to a mindless pleasure unlike anything she'd ever known.

"Zoe, baby, come! Come for me. Now!"

And she did, feeling him bucking with his own release as she felt all the wonder of the universe coalesce in her mind and body for one timeless moment.

Afterward, she lay under him, completely undone.

Zoe woke to the delicious sensation of Grant's warmth surrounding her. She snuggled closer, enjoying the feeling of rightness being in his arms engendered. He was sleeping soundly. Poor man. She had worn him out. She smiled with satisfaction. She had never felt this intimate with anyone before.

The only thing that marred her perfect happiness this morning was the realization that she and Grant had started an affair last night, not a forever. A small voice that would not be silenced taunted her with the idea that a future together was not such an impossible scenario. She wasn't supposed to want that. She'd meant this to be about sex.

But after what they had shared she could no longer deny that, far from being a clinical satiation of her sexual drive, last night had been the culmination of nearly a lifetime of loving. She was one hundred percent, head over heels in love with Grant. But she still wasn't sure she could trust him with her heart. He'd explained *The Night.* He'd even explained why he'd asked Carlene out, and both explanations had made sense.

If Grant didn't love her, if his desire for her was the physical thing she'd tried to convince herself hers had been, then it would make sense that he'd wanted to protect her from his "evil lust", as he'd put it. He wouldn't have wanted to hurt her by making love to her and eventually moving on, but she'd made it clear she was open to a physical relationship with him and, like he'd said, he hadn't been able to help himself any longer.

She didn't know what he felt about the future and, like an ostrich with her head buried in the sand, did not want to ask. What if she were right and he only wanted a friendly passion between the two of them? She'd rather deal with a broken heart down the road than now. If she waited to find out, she could enjoy the time they shared now, and maybe, just maybe, that time would bring Grant to a realization that he was as deeply in love with her as she was with him.

Their giving into the attraction between them had happened so abruptly that she still felt like she was in the aftermath of a tailwind. She definitely wasn't prepared to force a "relationship discussion" with Grant.

She slid reluctantly from the bed. She would like nothing better than to stay in bed with him for the rest of the day, but they needed to get his house cleaned up before his parents arrived from Portland. She also wasn't sure she had the *savoir-faire* to handle a naked-between-the-sheets morning after. She tiptoed to the closet and pulled out jeans, T-shirt and an oversized flannel shirt she had pilfered from Grant's closet sometime last summer.

She took a quick shower, not wanting to use up all the hot water. Grant would have to shower, and they needed to get a move on.

She smiled when she thought of the Cortezes' arrival. Having them around for Christmas would help make up for her own parents' defection. She dried her hair and pulled it back in her typical French braid, leaving some wisps to frame her face. After making coffee, she padded back to the bedroom in bare feet, carrying a mug of the steaming brew for Grant.

He was sitting on the side of the bed when she walked in. He grabbed the sheet and yanked it across his lap. She smiled at his modesty, even though she was sure she would have done the same thing herself. "A little late for that, isn't it?"

The smile he gave her in return looked a little forced. "Maybe."

If he was already regretting giving in to his desire for her she was going to scream—and not with pleasure like she had last night.

"I'll leave you alone to shower." She set the coffee on the table next to the bed. "This will help you wake up."

"Thanks."

She couldn't resist. She leaned forward to kiss him lightly on the lips before leaving the room. He averted his face and she ended up kissing the stubble on his chin instead. Zoe's insides froze. Last night had been a mistake. She could see it in the wary way he watched her.

She straightened and moved away from him. "I left you plenty of hot water, but you might want to make your shower quick. The faster we get to your house, the sooner we'll have everything cleaned up and ready for your parents."

She turned around and started from the room, ignoring him when he called her name. No tears came. Nothing. Just frozen pain. The way she'd felt when her dad had told her he'd sold the ranch and her parents were moving to Arizona to retire. Ranchers did not retire. But men who had lost their only son and heir, who saw their daughter as a complete write-off, did.

Grant's grip on her arms was the first inkling she had that he had followed her out of the bedroom. He spun her around to face him, every glorious naked inch of him. "What is going on?" Fury laced his words.

She felt the pain building. "You tell me."

"This is not a game, Zoe. Last night you went wild in my arms, and now you're walking away from me like I'm a cow pie on your boot."

"You promised." She glared at him, fighting the urge to cry. "You don't even remember, do you? You were just so hot, you said whatever you had to say so I wouldn't stop."

The dull red on his cheeks confirmed her suspicion like nothing else could. She struggled for release. "Let me go."

"No. Explain what you mean by my promise."

"You promised you would not regret what we did last night."

"You think I regret it?"

She searched his face, her conviction wavering. "Are you trying to tell me you don't?"

"Hell, no." His thumbs started a slow circling on her upper arms and she had to concentrate hard to remember what they were arguing about.

"But you turned your head when I tried to kiss you."

He closed his eyes and she had the distinct impression he was counting to ten. "Why weren't you in bed with me when I woke up this morning?"

She felt her face grow warm. "We need to get over to your house to get the place cleaned up before your parents arrive."

"Actually, we don't. I called an electrician and a cleaning crew out last night before I left to come here. But what has that got to do with you leaving the bed without waking me?"

"I thought if I took a shower first, we could get back to your place all that much faster." That hadn't been the only reason, and it must have shown on her face because he looked skeptical.

"And?"

She swallowed. "And I've never woken up naked with a man before. I didn't know how it was done."

"I'm not just any man, Zoe. I'm your best friend, and now I'm also your lover."

She craned her neck to meet his blue-eyed gaze. It was better than staring at his totally tantalizing naked body. "It's the lover part that I find a little disconcerting."

He reached out and held her shoulders, his expression grim. "Are you regretting last night?"

"No."

He leaned down and kissed her. "Good."

"So we both don't regret it?"

He kissed her again, this time with a little more passion. "Right."

"So why didn't you kiss me earlier?"

It was his turn to look chagrined. "I was mad when I woke up alone, and I thought you might be looking for a way to tell me last night was a mistake."

She laughed, and felt warmth cascade through her. He really did not regret making love to her. "I was just trying to be conscientious about getting back to your place before your parents got there."

"And shy."

She grinned in acknowledgement of his astute observation. "And a little shy."

He smiled and released her. "I'm going to take a shower. Why don't you pack while I'm at it?"

"Why?" She let her gaze roam down his naked body and felt the air leave her lungs in one big whoosh. His entire body was taut and hard.

"We might as well take your stuff to the ranch this morning." He talked as if standing around conversing naked, and with an obvious erection, was nothing out of the ordinary for him.

Heck, it probably wasn't. "What do you mean?"

"There's no point in you staying here, honey."

She bit her lip. "I can't move in with you, Grant."

He smiled again, this time with a definite glint in his eye. "My parents will be there. That's sufficient chaperonage in anybody's books."

"I don't want to flaunt an affair in your parents' faces."

"Affair?" His eyes darkened dangerously and he moved toward her, resolve written in every feature of his face.

Evidently he had a problem with the word *affair*. Maybe the word sounded too cheap to him. "Relationship. Whatever. I don't want your mom and dad thinking badly of me."

He stopped, his bare body inches from her. He didn't seem the least bit embarrassed by the fact his rather impressive male flesh brushed her stomach. "They're not going to think badly of you."

"They will if they find out we're sleeping together, and they'll want to know when the wedding is."

They would also tell her parents, who would then do one of two things. Demand to know when the wedding was to take place as well, or express their disappointment in a daughter who would make love to a man without the benefit of marriage. Maybe even both.

She didn't want to deal with either scenario. She also didn't want Grant put under that kind of pressure. If he decided they had a future together, it would be because he couldn't imagine his life without her—not because his parents and hers had guilted him into it.

"And we aren't planning on a wedding, right?" His voice was laced with an indefinable emotion. It sounded almost as if he were angry, but he had no reason to be.

She touched his arm in a conciliatory gesture. "Right."

His expression was serious and a little frightening as he bent and hooked one arm under her knees while using the other to support her shoulders.

She was airborne before she could gather her wits enough to demand, "What do you think you're doing?"

"Giving in to my instincts."

That was it. That was all he said as he carried her into

the bedroom. He didn't talk again. Not while he kissed her senseless as he stripped her clothes from her body; not while he aroused her in ways he hadn't even done the night before. He said nothing as he brought her to one shattering climax after another, but she said plenty. A lot of *pleases, Grants,* and even swearwords and demands she'd blush about later.

They didn't make it to his house for another three hours.

CHAPTER TWELVE

"EUDORA GIVENS evicted you this close to Christmas?" Roy Cortez's voice boomed with a condemnation that for some reason Zoe could not fathom rang a little false.

She watched him, trying to figure out why his eyes expressed something that looked like satisfaction while his mouth voiced censure. He and Lottie had arrived from Portland an hour after Grant and Zoe had made it back to the Double C, and Grant had just finished telling them about her eviction.

"I can't believe it."

Zoe smiled at Lottie's words. "Large dogs intimidate her, and she positively hates rodents. She freaked out when she found Bud in the bathroom."

"Bud?" Roy's angular face, so like his son's, creased in amusement. "You say he's a hamster?"

"That Grant gave you?" Lottie wasn't looking at Zoe.

Her entire attention and disapproving frown was settled on her stepson. An inch shorter than Zoe, the older woman's regard still managed to bring a sting of red up Grant's throat and into his cheeks.

"Yes." The word carried a wealth of guilt, which stung Zoe's own conscience.

"The hamster wouldn't have been such a big deal if I wasn't already four pets over my one pet quota."

"You wouldn't have any fool quota for your pets if you'd let Grant rent your old house to you." Roy shook his head as he shifted his tall frame on Grant's living room couch, moving infinitesimally closer to Lottie.

Zoe took a sip of the Christmas blend coffee Lottie had brought with her and insisted on making when they arrived. The subtle cinnamon flavor teased her tastebuds as she prepared to defend her decision not to rent her old home from Grant yet again. She wasn't taking charity from Grant and that was that. "I can't afford the rent a house like that would command."

Roy glared at her, his expression so like his son's Zoe couldn't help an internal smile. "Grant wouldn't have charged you more than you could afford. He'd have been happier if you would have taken the house as a gift, like he wanted you to in the first place."

Zoe grimaced, but held onto her temper. It wasn't Roy Cortez's fault he saw the world through the eyes of independent wealth. "Bottles of expensive perfume are gifts. Houses are not."

Grant frowned at his father. "Zoe didn't want the house."

Zoe stifled an urge to sigh. Grant was wrong. She *had* wanted the house, and the security it represented, but she'd had to prove she could make it on her own. If her own parents could cut her loose, she couldn't rely on the Cortezes to take care of her.

"That's right, Roy. Leave the poor girl alone. She's independent, and we wouldn't want you any other way," Lottie said as she smiled gently at Zoe.

Roy shrugged. "Stubborn too, but I still say Grant would

have felt a whole lot better if Zoe'd taken the house. He felt pretty bad, advising Jensen to sell."

Zoe felt as if everything inside her had gone still. She turned to meet Grant's wary blue gaze. "You *told* my dad to sell the ranch?"

He'd never said. Neither had her dad. Not that *that* surprised her.

"Yes."

"Did you also advise him to sell it without telling me first? Without giving me a chance to talk to him about it?"

It was Grant's turn to grimace, his gorgeous blue eyes reflecting frustration. "No. I didn't tell him to make the sale without talking to you first. But what would you have said, *niña*? You couldn't run it."

Ignoring Roy's interested gaze, and Lottie's sympathetic one, Zoe demanded, "How do you know?"

Grant's expression said it all. He knew—just like her dad had known. "Come on, Zoe. You never wanted to be a rancher. You're a kindergarten teacher and you love it." He leaned forward in his chair, tension vibrating off him. "Can you honestly say you would be happier trying to run the ranch?"

Of course not. But that wasn't the point. "If my brother had lived, you can bet my dad wouldn't have sold off the land and house without talking it over with *him* first."

Grant sighed. "If your brother had lived, your dad wouldn't have sold the ranch at all. But—"

She broke in before he could go on. "But he didn't live and my dad was stuck with me. I flunked at being a rancher's daughter and he knew I'd fail at running the ranch as well."

Pain coalesced inside Zoe as so many unmet needs rang hollowly through her soul. She had needed her father's unconditional acceptance, but she'd never gotten it. She'd needed to know she counted for something in her family besides the "oops" baby that had grown into the incomprehensible child. Those needs had never been met, and now Grant was telling her he'd been a part of one the most painful experiences of her life—her parents' final rejection.

They had sold her childhood home, bought property in Arizona, and waited to tell her until everything was a done deal.

Grant trapped her gaze with his own. "When you were six, you took a cow you'd befriended out on the range to save it from the stock sale. When you were nine, you buried the branding irons in your mother's garden. When you were thirteen, you opened the gates on the cattle-holding pens that had been marked for beef. You became a vegetarian when you were sixteen and you refused to come home from college for Spring Break your freshman year because it coincided with spring roundup."

She couldn't deny a single one of his charges.

He sighed, pain she did not understand reflecting in his eyes. "This isn't about failing. It's about wanting you to be happy—and your dad knew it wouldn't be running a ranch."

Grant stood up and moved toward her. He looked like he was going to touch her and she couldn't bear it. She jumped up. "I need to get back to the house. I've got presents that still need wrapping." And she desperately needed time to think—to come to terms with Grant's role in her dad's decision. "I'll leave the cats here for now, if you don't mind."

He put his hand out to grab her, but she evaded him and rushed from the room.

* * *

Grant wanted to shoot something, and his dad, sitting next to Lottie and looking so calm, made a likely target. "Why the hell did you have to tell her I advised Jensen to sell?"

"I didn't know it was a state secret."

Grant gritted his teeth. "It wasn't. It was something Zoe didn't need to know and clearly won't understand."

"Maybe you should try explaining it to her again, when she's had a chance to calm down." Lottie laid a hand on his dad's forearm. "And maybe *you* should learn to leave well enough alone."

His dad shook his head. "I've left well enough alone long enough. It hasn't gotten me one step closer to being a grandfather. Jensen neither."

Lottie groaned. "I should have known. So, you think putting their friendship at risk is going to catapult them into each other's arms?"

"It's worth a try. Jensen selling his ranch and leaving his daughter homeless sure as hell didn't do the trick."

Grant experienced a glimmer of understanding at his dad's belligerent words, along with more than a glimmer of aggravation. "Are you saying Zoe's dad sold the ranch to me as a way to bring the two of us together?"

His own father shrugged. "I'm not saying anything. But it's what I would have done if it had been left up to me."

Aggravation grew to anger. "And causing a major disagreement between Zoe and me is *your* idea of match-making?"

"It's time you two stopped dancing around each other and figured out the reason I don't have any grandchildren is because my son is in love with his best friend and too blind to see it."

Grant controlled the urge to yell. "I'm not blind."

It was his dad's turn to look enlightened. "So you figured out you loved her, did you?"

"I don't know about love, but I care about her."

"Hell, what else would you call it, boy?"

Grant remained stubbornly mute.

"Are you seeing each other again?" Lottie asked.

"We never stopped seeing each other."

"You know what I mean. Are you dating?"

After last night there could only be one answer to that question. "Yes."

His dad frowned. "So, what's the problem?"

"Don't you mean problems?" Grant sighed. "Zoe hated being a rancher's daughter. Really hated it. She was miserable on the ranch. But I belong here. And when I'm not here, I live in a world that doesn't impress her much either. She's a small-town girl, but not a rancher, and I'm not sure where that leaves us. Added to that, you've got her so mad at me I'm not sure she'll ever speak to me again."

"Are you sleeping with her, son?"

Tension arced right up Grant's spine and landed behind his eyes as a pulsing headache. Zoe was going to kill him, but she'd have to get him out of jail first, after he'd strangled his dad. "That's none of your business."

"I agree." Lottie's voice held the firm authority Grant had learned to respect as a child, and he knew his father didn't dismiss it lightly either. "Whatever is happening between the two of them is just that—between the two of them. I think you and Mr. Jensen have done enough."

His dad opened his mouth to speak, but closed it again at one look from Lottie's usually gentle gray eyes, now gone hard as slate. She turned her attention to Grant.

"Have you asked yourself what the ranch would mean to you if you lost Zoe because of it?"

"You mean like my dad had to do when you demanded he choose between you and his life as a rancher? He wouldn't give up the land for my mother, but he did for you, and, yes…maybe I'm beginning to understand how he could have made that choice."

But it wasn't one Grant wanted to make.

His dad leveled a look of censure at him. "Lottie may have made me choose between the ranch and her, but she didn't do it because she couldn't stand living the life of a rancher's wife."

"Then why did she do it?" Grant asked.

"I did it because your father was running his health into the ground, trying to run both the Cortez ranch holdings and his business ventures in Portland. He had a heart attack a couple of months before I gave him my ultimatum. It was a mild one, but the doctor told him something had to give."

Grant felt sucker punched and glared at his dad. "Why didn't you tell me?"

"I didn't want you to feel pressured into coming home from the east coast. You had your plans, and I wasn't going to ruin them, but then Lottie left for Portland and told me I could follow or be divorced."

"I meant it too." Lottie's eyes filled with a militant gleam. "I wasn't going to stick around to watch your father work himself into an early grave. Nothing was worth his health—not the ranch, nothing."

Grant couldn't argue with that. Lottie was right. His dad's health was more important than his former life-style, and Zoe was more important to Grant than his current one.

Nothing was worth losing Zoe. Not the ranch, nothing. Hell, it had to be love…nothing else could feel this damn scary.

As she drove toward the Pattersons', Zoe's mind kept replaying her conversation with Grant and his parents.

Grant had advised her dad to sell, and she couldn't blame him. Not when she thought about it rationally. He had been right. She didn't want to be a cattle rancher, and selling the ranch had been the only alternative that made sense for her parents. What he and her parents didn't seem to understand was her need to have been part of the decision—to have been legitimized as an important part of her family.

But that had not been Grant's choice. She clutched the cold steering wheel tightly, missing the gloves she'd forgotten to put on…again. She shouldn't have run out of Grant's house without talking out Roy's revelation. She'd left Grant believing she blamed him for her dad's rejection, and she didn't. She didn't even blame her dad. Losing his only son had broken something inside him and she'd never been able to fix it.

And she had to give her dad some credit. She had been a difficult child for a rancher to raise. She smiled at the memories Grant had brought up. She'd been too attached to the animals, and she'd spent hours drawing and writing stories when she was supposed to be doing chores.

It wasn't Grant's fault her parents didn't see her as a contributing member of their family unit either. But frankly that old pain had been well and truly superceded by a new one. Grant's advice to her dad only confirmed the lack of any hope for a future between them. He wasn't going to marry a woman who'd failed so miserably at the whole ranching lifestyle.

He might not realize it, but she knew he had major baggage left over from the three most important women in his life abandoning him for his lifestyle. He wouldn't risk marriage to someone who couldn't love him more than she hated ranching.

Zoe had spent the last four years running from her love for Grant, but she wasn't going to run any longer. She loved that stubborn rancher-tycoon more than anyone or anything else on earth, and she believed he loved her. He couldn't have made love to her the way he had otherwise. It had been too reverent…too spiritual. It had not been simple lust.

She would live in a snakepit if it meant being his wife. Telling him she wanted to share his life on a working cattle ranch was nothing in comparison.

She smiled with grim purpose as she turned into the Pattersons' drive. She had plans. The Christmas wrapping would have to wait. Grant had invited her to spend the holidays at the ranch, and she intended to accept his invitation.

Grant stood under the pulsing hot water, steam billowing around him, and closed his eyes.

Zoe had come back. She'd shown up on his doorstep not two hours after she'd left. She'd come in through the front door again. There was significance in that, but he didn't know what. She'd had all of her stuff too, not just a suitcase.

He'd wanted to yank her into his arms and kiss her until neither of them could breathe, but she'd made it clear she didn't want to flaunt the physical side of their relationship in front of his parents. He would heed her wishes, but as soon as the household had gone to sleep he was going to Zoe's room—even if it meant tiptoeing down a dark hallway.

He reached for the soap and touched a feminine hand instead. "Let me do that."

He spun around at the sound of the soft female voice and ran into a lot more female flesh. Naked female flesh. He opened his eyes and blinked. He rubbed them and blinked again. He still couldn't see anything. "Zoe?"

Soft, soapy hands started gliding over his torso. "Who else would accost you in the shower?"

"No one." He reached out to touch her, trying to see her tantalizing body in the inky blackness. "What happened to the lights?" His hand connected with resilient flesh and he cupped her breast, reveling in the feeling of her turgid nipple against his palm.

Her breath hitched and her hands started kneading his chest. "I turned them off. I wanted it to be just you and me. Nothing else. Not even the light." She moved a step closer and their bodies contacted from chest to knee.

He shuddered, feeling his hardened flesh press against the slick wet skin of her stomach. *"Querida—"*

She cut him off with a kiss, her lips sliding against his wet ones with erotic purpose. And just like that he gave up trying to figure out why the room had gone dark, or why Zoe had come to him at the risk of being caught out by his parents. He didn't care.

He kissed her with reckless male passion and caressed her back, then brushed his hands over her bottom, pressing her closer into his male heat. The dark lent a touch of un-reality to their lovemaking. Talk about male fantasy. He'd take Zoe's version any day of the week.

They were alone in a world of their own, where ranches

and cattle sold for beef had no place. Where no one and nothing could separate them. Where the past had no power to hurt and the present was nothing more than two bodies pressed close together in a darkness no light was allowed to penetrate.

Brushing the wet and curling hair on his chest, she shifted her legs apart until she straddled one of his thighs. He gave an involuntary groan at the first contact between her feminine juncture and his hair-roughened thigh. She caught her breath, tearing her lips from his to suck in more humid air, and moved experimentally against him. Sensation shot through him as he felt a wetness on his thigh that had nothing to do with the hot water cascading over them.

"Grant." His name coming out of the darkness in her voice, rough with passion, shivered along his senses like a caress.

She moved again, and made a startled sound when he lifted his leg and tightened his grip on her bottom, pressing her sensitive flesh more firmly against his thigh. "Do you like that, baby?"

"I…" Her voice trailed off as he moved his leg again, and she shuddered, crying out with irresistible feminine passion.

He had thought making love with her the first time had been the most mind-altering experience he could possibly have, but this wasn't just amazing—this was soul-transforming.

"Give it to me, Zoe. I want it all." He punctuated each word with a movement of his thigh, rejoicing as the sensitive skin against his thigh swelled and went silky smooth with wetness. "That's right, *niña.*"

"Please, Grant. You can have anything."

He stopped moving, his hands gripping her so tightly part of his conscious mind warned him about bruising her. "Anything?"

"Yes! Anything, Grant. Anything!" She tried to move on him again, but he wouldn't let her.

Instead he kissed her, a soft warm caress that felt like the sealing of something incredibly important. "Can I have your love? Will you give that to me?"

He waited in an agony of need, knowing her answer was more important to him than the desire clamoring for satiation.

Her hands came out of the darkness to cup his face. "I love you, Grant. I always have. I always will."

His body went rigid, and in a convulsive move he crushed her to him, spreading her legs more widely until he'd speared her with his hard maleness, giving them both what they craved. "I love you, Zoe. I will love you forever."

He pressed her against the shower wall, warm and slick from the hot spray, and drove into her with almost frightening intensity. He needed to slow down, but he couldn't. Her avowal of love had torn away his control, leaving only a primitive need to confirm that love in the most elemental way possible.

She didn't seem to mind as she hooked her legs around his waist, opening herself up completely to him. He drove into her with a circling motion, pressing the swollen bud of her pleasure against his pelvic bone with every thrust.

"I want to go so deep you can't remember what it's like not to be joined with me."

She gripped his shoulders with fingers like talons. "Yes!"

He made love to her with his entire body, his hands busy holding and touching her, his lips all over her face and neck, his chest rubbing her hardened nipples until she was screaming with pleasure and convulsing around him with one pulsing contraction after another.

He shouted as his release came over him, feeling one with her in a way he'd only ever known when his body was joined with Zoe's. He held her tightly to him as their breathing returned to normal. She kept her legs tightly wound around his waist.

"Ninety years of this is not going to be enough."

"Ninety years?" she asked, her voice sounding uncertain.

He kissed her forehead and gently disentangled their limbs, before pulling her back into the shower and washing her body with reverent care and a thoroughness that led her to another shattering explosion of physical sensation. When he finally turned the water off and pulled her from the shower, she held onto him like she needed his support to stay upright, while he groped in the dark for a towel.

He dried her off, kissing her body between tender swipes with the towel. She returned the favor, and it was all he could do not to initiate another bout of loving in the steam-filled room. He went to turn on the light.

"No. Don't."

"Baby?"

"There's something I want to say."

"And you want to do it while it's dark?"

He heard a soft sigh. "Yes. I don't want distractions or interruptions. Only the words. I want you to hear the words and believe them. Will you do that, Grant? Will you believe my words in the darkness?"

She sounded on the verge of tears, and he couldn't help reaching out to touch her. He found her arm, and from there settled both hands on her shoulders. "Yes. I'll believe anything you tell me, whether it's dark or not."

Her hands settled against his chest like the fluttering wings of a sparrow. "I love you."

"I love you, too."

One of her hands left his chest, and then he felt her finger tracing his lips, silencing them. "Thank you." Her shoulders rose and fell as she took a deep breath. "I know you think I can't be happy on a working ranch."

He nodded. Her fingers were still pressing his lips closed. "You're wrong."

He reached up and gently pulled her hand away from his mouth. "What are you trying to say?"

"Living with you, loving you, will make me happy. Living without you would be hell. Please don't make me do it."

He pulled her into a tight embrace. "Never. I want to marry you. I want you to have my babies. I'm not the one who started talking about affairs instead of a future after the most passionate night of love between two people known to man."

He reached over and flipped on the light. "Marry me, Zoe." He cupped her face with one hand while the other held her close to him. "I love you more than the ranch, more than my freedom, more than anything in my life. Marry me."

Her eyes filled with tears. "I love you. I love you so much. I'll live on the ranch with you. I'll have your babies, and I'll be as stoic as they come every year at the stock sale."

He smiled and shook his head, covering her lips with his thumb when she opened her mouth to answer. "I'd give up the ranch, if that was what it would take to make you happy as my wife, but I don't think I'll have to."

She nodded her head in agreement. "You don't have to."

How he loved this woman. She would do it. She would live a lifestyle she hated to be with him, and he knew deep down in his gut that she would never ask him to leave it for her sake. Zoe's love wasn't like that. She gave with both hands.

"We've got a couple of alternatives. We can venture into horse ranching. I've thought about raising Arabians before, but the cattle always required too much of my time."

Her brown eyes grew round and big. "Horses?" she whispered against his thumb.

"Yes. Or breeding cattle. They aren't sold for beef. What do you think?" He moved his thumb so she could answer.

The tears in her eyes spilled over, but her smile left no doubt in his mind that they were tears of joy. "I think loving you is the greatest gift I've ever had in my life."

"And loving you makes my life a gift." He crushed her mouth under his, knowing in his heart that even if he had to sell the ranch he would always be happy and complete as long as he had Zoe by his side.

CHAPTER THIRTEEN

ZOE sat in perfect stillness as she soaked in the feeling of rightness surrounding her. Her parents weren't here, but this was still the best Christmas she could ever remember.

The pastor had announced her and Grant's upcoming wedding at the Christmas morning service, and her principal had looked very relieved. She allowed a small smile to curve her lips.

"What's so funny, angel?"

Grant walked into the room with his dad, who carried the camcorder. Lottie was right behind them.

They'd already gorged on Christmas dinner, and now the time had come to open gifts. Next to church, this was Zoe's favorite part of the day. "I was just remembering the look of abject relief on my principal's face when the pastor announced our imminent wedding."

Grant grinned. "He doesn't have to worry about having another talk with you, huh?"

She smiled in return. "Uh-uh."

He moved to sit next to her on the sofa and put one arm around her shoulder, hugging her to his body. "Ready to open your presents?" he asked in a husky whisper against her ear.

She shivered in sensual response. "Do any of them come

packaged in fancy Spanish dye-tooled boots, well-worn jeans and red flannel?" she asked, describing his current attire.

He kissed her temple. "Not yet, *querida*, but soon."

She affected disappointment, but secretly thrilled to the anticipation he was building for their wedding night. He'd refused to make love again until they were married. She hadn't argued—not after he'd pointed out that they'd forgotten precautions in the shower and that he'd prefer their children were conceived after the wedding and not before.

Just then the doorbell rang, and Lottie left the room to answer it. Zoe was wondering who would be calling on Christmas Day when a familiar deep voice boomed from the entry hall.

"It's colder than a witch's tit out there."

Zoe sat paralyzed as her parents walked into Grant's living room. "You came."

"'Course we came," her dad said. "It's Christmas, ain't it?"

"Yes." It was Christmas, and her parents had come. She smiled at them. "I'm so glad to see you."

Her mother smiled warmly back, but her father actually walked right up to her and pulled her from the loveseat for a hug. "Glad to see you too, Zoe."

Her dad held her so tightly she could barely breathe, and he whispered two words into her ear she'd never expected to hear. "I'm sorry."

The pain of a lifetime couldn't be eradicated with a hug, but a lot of healing could happen—and did. Her mom pulled her into an embrace before Zoe could respond, but she squeezed her dad's arm as she let go of him.

Zoe turned to Grant. "Did you know they were coming?"

He nodded, and something in his eyes told her that he'd had something to do with it. He'd told her about their dads' attempts at matchmaking. Learning her dad had sold the ranch to Grant expecting it to pave the way for them to marry had helped detract from the lingering pain at the way he'd handled it.

She smiled at Grant, letting her love shine through. She mouthed the words for him alone.

I love you.

He put his hand out and drew her to him. "I love you, too, angel."

She sighed, and snuggled against him.

They were married on New Year's Day.

The church stood bright and beautiful in the winter sunshine, acting as a beacon as Grant walked through the side entrance, anticipation zinging through his body. Today Zoe would become his wife. He listened to the cacophony of voices and figured the majority of Sunshine Springs had turned out on short notice to witness his and Zoe's wedding.

A hush fell over the assembly, and the minister motioned Grant to take his place at the front of the church. Grant looked out over the crowded pews and smiled at their guests. Jenny and Tyler sat next to each other, their hands entwined. Grant's parents occupied the first pew to his right. Zoe's parents sat in the corresponding pew across the aisle.

Remembering Zoe's emotional reaction to her parents showing up at Christmas brought a smile to his face. She had cried when they arrived. She had cried again when he'd given her an engagement ring. For a woman who rarely wept, she had been very misty-eyed lately. He wondered if she would cry when she spoke her vows.

The "Wedding March" started and Grant fixed his eyes

on the back of the church. The guests stood, and then Zoe filled his vision. She wore her grandmother's wedding dress. It hadn't required any alterations, and the old-fashioned lace and veil suited Zoe to perfection. Grant's heart constricted at the sight, and he felt his hands twitching to touch her. She smiled at him and he knew that the radiant happiness he saw in her eyes was reflected in his own.

She reached his side and the minister instructed Grant to take her hand. He spoke his vows with assurance, gazing directly into her eyes. When he said, "I do," his voice sounded strong, as if he had been practicing all his life. He felt like he had.

A scream rent the air. Grant and Zoe both spun around to see what the commotion was about. Carlene stood on a pew at the back of the church, her peach-colored miniskirt visible above the heads of the couple in front of her.

"Rodents!"

Grant groaned. Zoe laughed, and a little boy, looking uncomfortable in his Sunday best, pushed his way into the center aisle. "That's no rodent. That's my hamster. He used be Miss Jensen's. He wanted to see the wedding too."

Surprised gasps and shrieks followed this announcement. Within seconds the entire church was a massive scene of pandemonium. Everywhere but the front two pews. Zoe's and Grant's parents remained in their seats.

"We're used to this sort of thing, pastor. We raised her." Zoe's father's words, spoken with resignation but some humor too, brought a smile to Grant's lips.

"The hamster?" the minister asked.

"No. Our daughter. Zoe."

Grant met Zoe's eyes, and they both burst into laughter. He turned back to the minister. "Go on."

The pastor rubbed his hand across his bald head. "You sure? Wouldn't it be better to wait until the rodent is found?"

Zoe shook her head. "That's not a rodent. It's Bud, and they'll find him eventually. Please go on."

Grant hoped they caught Bud before the hamster found his way into the church walls and its wiring.

The minister led Zoe in her vows. When it was her turn to speak, Zoe took a deep breath. Tears misted her eyes and Grant was pleased that he had been right. Her voice was husky and full of emotion when she made her promises.

Tyler shouted from behind Grant. *"I've got him."*

Grant looked back over his shoulder to see a small furry head peeking out from Tyler's fist. It seemed only right that Bud had witnessed their marriage. After all, he had been instrumental in bringing Grant to his senses where Zoe was concerned.

He turned back to his wife. *His wife.* Damn, that sounded good. From the look in her eyes, she felt the same way. They smiled and turned together to face the minister, who was muttering about most irregular events. The pandemonium in the church settled down, and the minister finished the ceremony and gave Grant permission to kiss Zoe.

Grant lowered his head and took Zoe's mouth in a kiss that sealed their future and their love.

REQUEST YOUR FREE BOOKS!

 HARLEQUIN® *Presents~* ®

 PASSION GUARANTEED SEDUCTION

2 FREE NOVELS PLUS 2 FREE GIFTS!

YES! Please send me 2 FREE Harlequin Presents® novels and my 2 FREE gifts. After receiving them, if I don't wish to receive any more books, I can return the shipping statement marked "cancel." If I don't cancel, I will receive 6 brand-new novels every month and be billed just $3.80 per book in the U.S., or $4.47 per book in Canada, plus 25¢ shipping and handling per book and applicable taxes, if any*. That's a savings of close to 15% off the cover price! I understand that accepting the 2 free books and gifts places me under no obligation to buy anything. I can always return a shipment and cancel at any time. Even if I never buy another book from Harlequin, the two free books and gifts are mine to keep forever.

106 HDN EEXK 306 HDN EEXV

Name _____ (PLEASE PRINT)

Address _____ Apt. #

City _____ State/Prov. _____ Zip/Postal Code

Signature (if under 18, a parent or guardian must sign)

Mail to the **Harlequin Reader Service®**:
IN U.S.A.: P.O. Box 1867, Buffalo, NY 14240-1867
IN CANADA: P.O. Box 609, Fort Erie, Ontario L2A 5X3

Not valid to current Harlequin Presents subscribers.

Want to try two free books from another line?
Call 1-800-873-8635 or visit www.morefreebooks.com.

* Terms and prices subject to change without notice. NY residents add applicable sales tax. Canadian residents will be charged applicable provincial taxes and GST. This offer is limited to one order per household. All orders subject to approval. Credit or debit balances in a customer's account(s) may be offset by any other outstanding balance owed by or to the customer. Please allow 4 to 6 weeks for delivery.

Your Privacy: Harlequin is committed to protecting your privacy. Our Privacy Policy is available online at www.eHarlequin.com or upon request from the Reader Service. From time to time we make our lists of customers available to reputable firms who may have a product or service of interest to you. If you would prefer we not share your name and address, please check here. ☐

HP07

*The Rich, the Ruthless
and the Really Handsome*

How far will they go to win their wives?

A trilogy by Lynne Graham

Prince Rashad of Bakhar, heir to a desert kingdom,
Leonidas Pallis, scion of one of Greece's leading dynasties
and Sergio Torrente, an impossibly charismatic,
self-made Italian billionaire.

Three men blessed with power, wealth and looks—
what more can they need? Wives, that's what…and
they'll use whatever means to take them!

THE DESERT SHEIKH'S CAPTIVE WIFE
by Lynne Graham
Book #2692

Rashad, Crown Prince of Bakhar, was blackmailing Tilda over
a huge family debt—by insisting she become his concubine!
But one tiny slipup from Rashad bound them together forever….

Read Leonidas's story in

THE GREEK TYCOON'S DEFIANT BRIDE
by Lynne Graham
Book #2700
Available next month!